Advance Praise for *Dump 'Em*

"This book tells how t[...] [...] Speyer's
engaging real-life storie[...] [...] being respectful when breaking [...] to be fair
and appreciative—no matter what. Readers will learn to handle
those awkward farewells with consideration and tact."

—Peggy Post, director of The Emily Post
Institute and author of *Emily Post's Etiquette,
17th Edition*, and *"Excuse Me, But I Was Next..."*

"*Dump 'Em* is not just funny, it's practical. Jodyne Speyer has
figured out a way to sever the ties that so many of us would
rather miserably live with forever."

—Sarah Silverman, comedienne

"Jodyne Speyer's *Dump 'Em* is surprising, practical and funny.
Or would be had it not reminded me of the wonderful time Jodyne and I had together before, well, the dumping."

—Jon Hamm, actor on *Mad Men*

"This book is so funny and smart and savvy I dumped my wife!
And I love my wife. I might have blown it."

—Greg Behrendt, author of *He's Just Not That Into You*

"A funny and practical guide to getting the people in your life
out of your life."

—Jimmy Kimmel, host of *Jimmy Kimmel Live*

"*Dump 'Em* is *my* guidebook to getting rid of people."

—Fran Drescher, actress

DUMP 'EM

DUMP 'EM

How to Break Up with Anyone from Your Best Friend to Your Hairdresser

JODYNE L. SPEYER

With Illustrations by Julie Bossinger

COLLINS LIVING
An Imprint of HarperCollins Publishers

The information in this book has been carefully researched, and all efforts have been made to ensure accuracy (meaning I did more than surf the Web. I went to libraries, spoke to professionals, and made tons of phone calls). The author and the publisher assume no responsibility for any injuries suffered or damages or losses incurred during or as a result of following this information. (So if you drop the book on your foot or someone decides to hit you with it, while you have my deepest sympathy, you're on your own.) All information should be carefully studied and clearly understood before taking any action based on the information or advice in this book.

HarperCollins books may be purchased for educational, business, or sales promotional use. For information, please write: Special Markets Department, HarperCollins Publishers, 10 East 53rd Street, New York, NY 10022.

FIRST EDITION

Designed by Jaime Putorti

Library of Congress Cataloging-in-Publication Data is available upon request.

ISBN 978-0-06-164662-1

09 10 11 12 13 OV/RRD 10 9 8 7 6 5 4 3 2 1

"Some cause happiness wherever they go;
others whenever they go."
—Oscar Wilde

contents

introduction

If there was an award for avoiding confrontation, I'd win it. I'm sure many of you think you might tie me, or dare say beat me, but I beg to differ. I've spent hours—okay, months—of my life coming up with excuse after excuse for getting out of everything from a simple hair appointment to casual drinks with friends. How do you tell a friend that you've made a terrible mistake, and to please forgive you . . . but you find her painfully boring? My solution was to avoid their calls and hope that they'd stop calling. I can now confidently report that this almost never works.

Deciding that I didn't want to be that person anymore, I went in search of a book to teach me how to dump people. I discovered thousands of books about ending romances, but none about how to leave the other people in our lives—many of whom we see on a daily basis—like our co-workers, our roommates, or our families. How do I break up with these people? Who would teach me?

I started by talking to friends, family, professionals, and other people who grappled with the very same problem, and I asked them, "How do you do it?" They shared horror stories of desperately wanting to dump their cleaning ladies, hairdressers, and therapists, then begged me to write this book.

So here I had all this useful information, but I still couldn't get over the hump of why me? Although I'm a writer, I'm by no means a how-to expert. And then I realized that for the most part, the feeling of dread that comes up when we have to dump someone is universal, and you don't have to be a doctor to know when a relationship is not healthy.

Weaving together personal stories, poetic license, practical tools, scripts for you to use, and interviews with actual experts, I have tried to give you all the tools you'll need for ending any bad relationship you may encounter.

I am grateful for the all-around smart people who provided guidance and advice, including everyone's favorite trainer, Bob Harper from *The Biggest Loser*; funnyman Adam Carolla; Michael Jackson's attorney, Thomas Mesereau; professional houseguest Kato Kaelin; and my sister Sarah Silverman, whom I told that if she didn't contribute, I would dump her.

DUMP 'EM

part one
UNSUPPORTIVE SUPPORT

one

THE HAIRDRESSER

Signs It's Time to Dump Your Hairdresser

▶ Your smock is covered in dandruff . . . and it's not yours.

▶ With each snip of her scissors, she grunts like a female tennis player.

▶ She's still stuck in the '80s. Who wants a perm?

▶ When you walk in, her last appointment is leaving in tears.

▶ You go in for a bang trim and leave missing an eyebrow.

Hair Today, Gone Tomorrow

While attending college in New York City, I got my hair cut at a trendy little boutique in the East Village. My hairdresser, Gina, was a plain Jane from Staten Island, and that was exactly what I liked about her. Unlike a lot of my previous hairstylists—who pretended to listen while they plotted to give me (usually successfully) the haircut they wanted—Gina actually listened to me and gave me the cut I asked for—which is why I was devastated when she told me that she was leaving for six months to go on a spiritual journey to India.

Within days of returning from her trip, I made an appointment at her apartment. Graduation was coming up and I wanted a new look. I raced up her stairwell two steps at a time, excited for the hairstyle that would take me to the next stage of my life: my career.

As I reached the top of her staircase, I nearly choked on the heavy cloud of incense smoke that invaded my lungs. The smell of Nag Champa overwhelmed me. Waving it away, I pushed open Gina's front door and entered what I can only describe as some kind of medieval dungeon filled with giant candelabras, enormous crosses, leering gargoyles, and black sheets draped over huge gothic columns. I should have turned around and left then; the smell of incense makes me want to vomit (I already had, just a tiny bit). Not to mention that goth scares me. It was so dark that I could barely see my feet—and if I couldn't see, how would Gina be able to cut my hair?

"Hello?" I shouted. Out of the darkness came Gina, fully covered in piercings, hair in long dreads, and wearing a black, free-flowing, Stevie Nicks–style dress. Who was this woman? This was not my Gina from Staten Island—Coney Island, perhaps.

What exactly did they teach her in that ashram? She made her move toward me.

"Jodyne! My queen! At last! I've waited my whole life for you!" Then she broke into a Mary J. Blige song. "My life. My life. My life. In the sunshine. If you look at my life, and see what I've seen." India had apparently turned Gina into a hippie goth—a gippie?—but that still didn't explain why she was singing Mary J. Blige to me. "Let's go, mamma!" she said as she grabbed my hand and led me to her sink.

My whole plan of talking to her first, going over my hair—the style, the number of inches and layers—all of it washed right down that sink of hers. I completely shut down. To make matters worse, I also couldn't see, because I had made the mistake of wearing my glasses instead of my contacts that day. Gina had taken my glasses and set them on top of one of her scary gargoyles. I was having a total out-of-body experience. I watched her cut my hair, was engaged in conversation, yet I don't remember anything I said. What I do remember is her saying things like, "I totally get it. I so know what to do with you. Oh, I just love giving people new looks. You're gonna love it!"—and then another Mary J. Blige song. "Ohhhhh, sweet thing. Don't you know you're my everything. Woe oh, hooooh, sweet thing."

Fast-forward twenty minutes. My smock came off, and I was staring at myself in the mirror. All I could see was a blurry cloud of incense smoke. I frantically grabbed my glasses, almost knocking the gargoyle off the table (which I suspect was actually a coffin). "Well, what do you think, rock goddess?" asked Gina. Staring back at me in the mirror was a complete stranger. I was speechless. I blinked my eyes five times to make sure it was me. It was me alright; me wearing a mullet. That's right, a mullet—I couldn't get away from that mirror fast enough.

I ran down Prince Street at lightning speed, pushing people

out of my way in order to get home as quickly as possible. It's a bird, it's a plane, it's—a mullet? As I sprinted past a crowd of people planted in front of Dean and Deluca, someone shouted, "Hey, Joan Jett!" And I'm pretty sure I also heard someone say, "Look, it's Andrew Ridgeley!" For those who don't know Andrew Ridgeley, he was one-half of the musical group Wham, along with George Michael. He also sported a mullet.

For the next week, I refused to go outside. I covered all the mirrors in my apartment and sat shiva. My friends stopped by and offered their condolences. They suggested that I go back to Gina to have her fix my hair before graduation. But how could I? That woman was not my Gina; something had happened to her in India. I called my parents and told them not to come to graduation. That phone call didn't go so well. My father pointed out that when parents fund their children's ridiculously expensive educations, it automatically gives them the right to attend their graduation ceremonies. They were coming, like it or not.

The day of graduation, Gina left a message on my cell, wishing me luck and hoping to hear how I liked the new me. I never called her back. More calls followed. I erased each message unheard. Apparently, the new me was a coward. My graduation was saved by my fashionable mother, who brought with her an assortment of scarves left over from her '70s *Rhoda* days. I had never been a scarf girl, but these were really something: all vintage, all fabulous. Luckily, the scarf was a huge hit at graduation. People not only asked where I had bought it, but wanted to take a picture of me. For the next six months, which was as long as it took for me to grow out my hair, I was a fashion icon of downtown New York. And Gina? I never saw her again, but I think of her every time I hear a Mary J. Blige song or see someone with a mullet.

What I Learned

I should have called Gina back, or at least picked up the phone when she called. It certainly would have made me feel better— after all these years, I still feel guilty about the way I treated her. She went out of her way for me that day and I bolted, out of her apartment and out of her life forever. There was talk about meeting for a drink so I could hear about her trip, but my childish behavior put an end to that.

One of the most valuable things I learned while writing this chapter is how important it is to be prepared before going to your hairdresser, especially if you're going to a new one. From cutting out pages from magazines to bringing in personal photographs of the hairstyle you want, it's up to you to communicate what you want to your hairdresser. I spoke to a woman in Manhattan who stops women on the street and asks them if she can take a picture of their haircut to show her hairdresser. Remember, your idea of what a person's haircut looks like might be totally different than your hairdresser's. Thinking back to Gina, I went to her apartment with nothing in hand. I put all the power in her hands to change my look just days before graduation. That was my mistake.

While it's important to listen to your hairdresser's suggestions about haircuts, at the end of the day, you're the one wearing the 'do—so speak up! Tell your hairdresser what kind of person you are: chill, high maintenance, conservative, liberal, rocker? Don't leave her guessing. A number of people I spoke to for this chapter confessed to being bullied by their stylists and ended up getting cuts that they hated. When I asked them whether they said anything to their hairdressers, very few said that they had. The reason? They were afraid to hurt their hairdressers' feelings. But you're paying for the haircut *you* want, not the haircut *she* wants you to have. Others said that it took them months to book the appointment with the new and hot stylist, so they didn't want to insult her. The best piece of advice I got while researching this chapter was how many salons offer free consultations. This is a great way of figuring out whether or not you like a potential hairdresser. Pay attention to whether or not *she* pays attention to *you*. Make sure she asks you the right questions, and be sure to tell her as much as you can about you and your hair. If you don't like the vibe, don't make an appointment—or be prepared to walk out with a mullet.

Laying the Groundwork

▶ Make sure you have realistic expectations of what your hair can and cannot do. If you don't know, ask your hairdresser.

▶ Start emotionally disengaging from your current hairdresser. Your goal is to slowly shift your relationship to a less personal, more professional one so that dumping her will be easier.

▶ Give your hairdresser a warning. Point out what you don't like about your hair. Be specific: Do you hate the length? Troubled by the color? Lost in the layers? Tell her.

▶ Find a new hairstylist. Stop people on the street who have hairstyles you like. Pick up beauty and hair magazines, such as *Allure* or *Celebrity Hairstyles*. If you need help, check out www.StylistMatch.com. The Web site has a search engine that finds hairdressers in your area who specialize in your hair type. When possible, they also provide you with pictures of local salons.

- Call salons around town and take advantage of free consultations.

- Rehearse what you're going to say to your current hairdresser.

How to Dump 'Em

Tip: For those of you who've become friends with your hairdresser, don't dump her by not showing up again. It may seem like the least confrontational route, but can easily lead to a highly charged run-in when you least expect it—at the market, the mall, your favorite restaurant, or the fragrance counter at Barneys. This happened to me with my old hairdresser, who was totally unpredictable with her cuts. There I was, alone and vulnerable, just wanting a new scent, when she cornered me and demanded that I tell her why I stopped going to her. She felt totally abandoned by me and was afraid that she had done something wrong. I was completely caught off guard and stuttered my way out of it, but I was so distraught that I ended up avoiding Barneys for a year. If you're not ready to speak honestly with your hairdresser, at the very least make up a white lie so that she doesn't feel abandoned.

TALK TO THE HAIR(STYLIST)

People—especially women—spend a great deal of time at the hair salon. A cut and color can easily take three hours. High-end hairstylists cater to their clients by offering them espresso drinks, wine, champagne, croissants, etc. It feels good to be taken care of by someone who wants nothing more than to make you look your very best. I've felt intoxicated upon leaving a salon; that could have been the alcohol, but still. To have a pair of professional hands work their magic and transform us into our most glamorous selves is pretty great. But all hairdressers go through rough patches, and some of them let their personal lives affect their work. If you've already laid the groundwork, you've been working on disengaging from your hairdresser. Remember, dumping her is business, not personal.

STEPS

1. **Stop by or call your hairdresser.**

2. **Acknowledge your discomfort:** *"This is an awkward conversation to have."*

3. **Identify the issues you've been having with your cuts.** *"As you know I haven't been wild about _____ these past few months."*

4. **Dump her.** *"We've tried a number of things to make this work, but I'm still not getting the results I was hoping for. This is difficult to say, but it's time for me to check out another hairdresser."*

5. **Allow your hairdresser to respond. Some might let their egos come into play (not your problem!)—others might ask for another chance. Think twice. If you decide to give her one more shot, make it clear that you mean one more haircut, period. The best-case scenario is that your hairdresser will support your decision. You might be surprised by how many hairstylists will be okay with you leaving. Most genuinely want you to be happy.**

6. **Thank her for everything.**

MUSICAL SALON CHAIRS

Many of the people I interviewed for this chapter had questions about how to handle the awkwardness involved when someone wants to see another hairstylist at the same salon. I spoke with a number of professionals, and most agreed that the way to handle it is to make your first appointment on your current hairdresser's day off. When you sit at the new hairdresser's chair, speak up and let her know that this is a trial appointment. If the new haircut is a success, leave a note for your old hairdresser at her station saying, "Stopped in and had my hair done with _____. Thanks for everything but I've decided to make the change to her." Then the next time you see your old hairdresser, make a point of going over and acknowledging her. It doesn't have to be much, just a quick wave hello. The one second of awkwardness will pass quickly, making for a much easier transition to the new stylist, and before you know it, the discomfort will disappear.

1-800-FLOWERS.COM

Still not sure how to dump your hairdresser? Send her flowers.

WHAT YOU CAN WRITE:

Dear _____,
Thank you for all your wonderful haircuts throughout the years. I've decided to take my hair in a new direction.
Sincerely,

_____

THE GIFT THAT KEEPS ON GIVING.

Still looking for an easy way out? Dump your hairdresser by telling her that you were given a very generous gift certificate to another salon. Mention a big promotion at work, a milestone birthday, or a wedding anniversary.

Bonus: This option allows you to keep the salon door open should you wish to return in the future.

In a Pinch

LOCKS OF LOVE
Guess who's growing their hair out? You are! Tell your hairdresser that you've committed to donating your hair to Locks of Love, a nonprofit organization that gives hairpieces to disadvantaged children under the age of eighteen who are suffering from medical hair loss. The minimum hair length it accepts is ten inches. Another option is to mention how much you love, love, love Rapunzel's or Fabio's hair, and wish you had long hair. Tell her that you've made the decision to just go for it—grow it out once and for all. If she offers to trim it for you, let her know that her prices are too high for what you need right now. She shouldn't expect to see you for years.

LICE, LICE, LICE, YEAH
Tell your hairdresser that you've picked up a bad case of head lice and had to shave your hair off. The good news is that you actually like it and are trying to decide whether to keep it that short or grow it out; either way, you won't be seeing her for a while.

Q. *How do you know when it's time to dump your hairdresser?*
A. If you crack open that old high school photo album and your hair still looks the same, you're in trouble!

Q. *How do you dump your hairdresser?*
A. You know what works for me? A card wishing me the best of luck in my future and career.

Q. *What's the best way to tell your hairdresser that you don't like the cut she just gave you?*
A. First, don't try and play passive aggressive by saying, "I like it, but—." Be honest and direct. We're there to make you happy. Tell us, or bring a picture of the cut you wanted and show us what you like about the picture that you don't see with your hair. Be firm, polite, and to the point. If the cut is less than one month old, go to your hairstylist and ask them for a redo.

Q. *What should someone do if she feels that her hairdresser is bullying her into a cut?*
A. You're the one who has to live with it, not them, so speak up! Try "I'm sure it's a great hairstyle, but you'll just have to find another client for it, because it's not for me." Some hairdressers pick up ideas for cuts at hair shows and are overly anxious to try out those cuts on their clients, so be careful.

Q. *What's the biggest mistake you think hairdressers make with their clients?*
A. They dismiss their clients' taste by imposing their own. Hopefully they at least have taste, but still, you want a hairstylist who listens. Another mistake is when they give the same cut to everyone.

Q. *What's the biggest mistake clients make with their hairdressers?*
A. When they become their friends. Your hairstylist is your "staff" with benefits. It's much better to keep things light. It's fine to invite them to parties or events, but keep things at a distance. Remember, hairstylists talk. Many say they will be discreet, but the moment you leave their chair, anything is game, including talking with your frenemies. So be very careful about unloading too much information, or making them your shrink.

Q. *What should someone who wants to see a new stylist at the same salon as their current one do?*
A. People need to stop feeling like they're cheating on their hairstylist. Think about it this way; it's no different than trying out a new restaurant. I would make an appointment on your hairstylist's day off, and if you happen to see your old hairstylist, be friendly, but remember—you don't have to justify yourself.

Q. *Do blondes really have more fun?*
A. Blondes have more fun, but they don't know it until it's too late and the fun is over. Brunettes never stop having fun; they know how to morph with time and be beautiful and graceful about it.

DUMPIPEDIA

▸ Singer Amy Winehouse dumped her hairdresser and close friend Alex Fodden, apparently as a result of pressure from her management company to distance herself from people seen as having a negative influence on her life.

▸ The average scalp has how many strands of hair?
  A. 10,000
  B. 100,000
  C. 1,000,000

▸ A blonde head of hair has more strands than red or dark hair.

▸ Danny DeVito used to work as a hairdresser at his sister's hair salon.

▸ The average life span of a strand of hair is between four and seven years.

The answer is B. 100,000.

two

THE MANICURIST/WAXER

Signs It's Time to Dump Your Manicurist/Waxer

▶ She waxes your fingers and paints your crotch.

▶ You go in for a manicure and she asks whether you want a "full release."

▶ Your eyebrows look like you just left a Star Trek convention.

▶ You go in for an eyebrow wax and she says, "What are we doing today, just the beard?"

▶ You ask for a landing strip and end up with a shamrock.

Ripping Her Right Out of Your Life

A few years ago, while flipping though the back pages of *New York* magazine, I stumbled upon an advertisement that read, "Got nails? Will travel. Private nail technician available for parties of eight or more. Discreet." A nail party sounded like a great way to spend time with my friends, so I made the call.

The following day, invitations were sent out and my first nail party was an instant success—so much so that it became a monthly event. Guys, gals, friends, friends of friends—they all came. Manicures, pedicures, wearable nail art: you name it and Jenny, my new nail technician, did it.

Even better, in addition to being great with nails, she also gave fantastic advice. It didn't take long before Jenny had become our therapist, and the next thing I knew, I was wandering the streets of New York City in times of crisis, asking myself, "What would Jenny tell me to do right now?" Even my friend Heather (who attended the nail parties) confessed that she too had called Jenny at home for some words of wisdom about her boyfriend.

Jenny loved it. She couldn't get enough of us looking to her for advice; that was the problem. She was so into playing Dr. Phil that the wisdom started flowing a little too freely. Although her ad claimed that she was "discreet," the truth was she was anything but—now blabbing about everyone's private business. When a male friend came with his new girlfriend (who had her manicure first), Jenny blurted out to him that he should "Stay away from her. She got the herpes." I don't know if she had changed her meds or whether it was just boredom, but Jenny suddenly had no censor. As for my friend who called Jenny at home to get advice about her boyfriend? She was thrown under the bus when

Jenny spilled the beans to her boyfriend during a manicure. "She don't love you no more. Having second thought." Another friend, Christina, confided in Jenny about the trouble she was having with her best friend's mood swings. Jenny then blabbed to that friend that Christina had called her "a real live Jekyll and that other bad dude."

Alas, as all good things must come to an end, so went the glory days of the nail parties. People were so pissed off at Jenny that they stopped coming, and I could no longer meet Jenny's minimum requirement. I was going to have to dump my beloved Jenny. I tried making new friends so that I wouldn't have to, but the damage was done. Jenny put her own foot (albeit a finely pedicured one) in her mouth. In the end, she was responsible for two romantic breakups, two best friend breakups, and one person getting fired.

What I Learned

You couldn't pay me to get my nails done at a salon today unless I knew beyond a shadow of a doubt that the place was completely sterile. This chapter was a total eye-opener for me; did you know that salons have reported transmission of herpes, hepatitis, nail fungus, loss of nails, and (in rare cases) AIDS? What's worse is that no one seems to be paying attention to the problem; I walked into nail salon after nail salon in New York and Los Angeles while researching this chapter and was absolutely floored to see how many of them didn't disinfect their tubs or instruments. From cheap salons on every corner of New York to high-end spas, very few actually cleaned their tools between clients, washed their hands, or changed their gloves. I walked into one salon and saw blood on the manicurist's clippers.

People aren't paying attention, and salon owners know this. How many of you know of salons that have Dremel files or callous scrapers hidden in drawers? Do any of you notice whose feet were soaking in the tub before you, or whether the manicurist or pedicurist cleaned the bowl or tub you put your hands and feet into? Scary, right? I never paid attention—until now. The *Boston Globe* recently reported that Massachusetts's health inspectors did a sweep of Newton, a wealthy suburb of Boston, and discovered that 42 percent of the 88 salons investigated were in violation of state sanitation regulations. The most common violations were unsanitary conditions, expired licenses, and unlicensed employees.

Today I bought my very own nail kit. In fact, I bought five of them to hand out to some of my closest friends in order to protect their nails. If one of my friends is reading this now and wondering why she didn't get one, you were out of town.

Laying the Groundwork

▶ Find a new manicurist/waxer. If you're looking for suggestions in your area, check out Allure.com and www.FindABeauty Salon.com to find a salon in your area, as well as look at photos, read reviews, and request an appointment.

▶ If you left a nail kit at your salon, get it back.

How to Dump 'Em

TALK TO THE HAND

Getting your nails done or having your hair waxed is an intimate experience. Manicurists hold your hands and feet for close to (if not longer than) an hour. Waxers work near the most private parts of your body. While it may be easy for those of you who don't go to a salon on a regular basis to walk away and never go back, it's not so easy for those living in a small town where you might bump into her in the neighborhood, or for those with ongoing appointments. In these cases, a phone call or a quick visit to the salon to let your manicurist or waxer know you're not coming back is in order.

STEPS

1. **Call your manicurist/waxer or stop by during a time when she's not busy.**

2. **Start with a compliment.** *"Thanks for _____ great years."*

3. **Dump her.** *"But with my crazy schedule, I need to go to a salon closer to home/work."*

4. **Thank her.** *"Thank you for everything. I'll miss our conversations."*

LICENSE REQUIRED

No license, no manicure. Make sure that your salon has a valid business license on display—if it says 1986, you're in trouble. Same goes for your nail technician. Be sure to look at the picture on the license! I once went to a nail salon and had my nails done by a woman named "May," but when I glanced at the license hanging on the wall behind her, I noticed the name and picture was of someone else named "Lynn." I asked her who Lynn was, and she responded, "Who?" Then it registered and she said, "Me! That's me." I never went back.

Since a majority of salons aren't properly inspected, you're at risk for serious infections and diseases such as hepatitis A, B, and C, nail fungus, or even HIV.

WHAT YOU SAY: *"I've been reading about all the infections and diseases out there and I'm really concerned. I'm sorry, but I absolutely must go to a manicurist who is licensed and a salon that is inspected regularly."*

BE PREPARED FOR HER TO SAY: *"I have a license. I must have lost it."*

FINAL WORD: *"I'm sorry: no license, no manicure."*

I HIRED A NEW MANICURIST/WAXER. ME!!!

With more and more nail and waxing products available at local drugstores, it's never been easier to bring the salon experience into your home. Dump your manicurist/waxer by telling her that there's a new kid on the block—you!

WHAT YOU SAY: *"I've decided to start doing my own nails. I've found that it saves time and money. Thanks for everything."*

BE PREPARED FOR HER TO SAY: *"Oh, no, you don't know how to do them. They're very difficult to do yourself."*

FINAL WORD: *"I didn't think I would be able to do it either, but it turns out that not only can I do it, I'm actually really good at it."*

NAIL PARTY!

Nail/waxing parties are a great way of socializing with friends. Tell your manicurist/waxer that you've decided to start hosting them at your house.

Bonus: This option leaves the salon door open in case you wish to return in the future.

WHAT YOU SAY: *"I've decided to start having nail/waxing parties at my house. Thanks for everything."*

BE PREPARED FOR HER TO SAY: *"I'd be careful if I were you. Most of the people who do nail parties are not professionals."*

FINAL WORD: *"If I run into problems, I'll let you know."*

WHAT YOU HOPE SHE DOESN'T SAY: *"How fun! Can I come?"*

GUESS WHO'S GETTING LASER HAIR REMOVAL?

There's no better time than the present to get rid of those unwanted hairs once and for all. Dump your waxer by telling her that you've decided to jump on the bandwagon.

ALL NATURAL

Walking into a nail salon can be like walking into an auto body shop; they use a lot of the same chemicals, just in smaller quantities. In fact, many of the chemicals in nail polish have been linked to cancer and birth defects. Don't believe me? Go online and see for yourself. To make matters worse, most salons don't have proper ventilation, which means that you are breathing in those toxic chemicals for as long as you stay in the salon. Dump your manicurist or waxer by telling her that you're going green. Then do yourself a favor and look around for a salon that uses natural, organic products.

In a Pinch

SURPRISE! GUESS WHO'S A HEALTH INSPECTOR!

Tell your manicurist/waxer that you're a health inspector. Let her know that she doesn't have to worry, that even though she is in violation of a number of codes, you're not going to write her up just as long as she promises to fix a few things. Don't like the water-stained artwork hanging on the wall? Add it to your list!

TEXT MESSAGE BREAKUP

It worked for Britney Spears, so let it work for you.

U+ME=THRU.

DUMPIPEDIA

▶ Paula Abdul dumped her manicurist when a bad manicure cost her a thumbnail.

▶ According to the *Guinness Book of World Records*, Lee Redmond of Salt Lake City holds the record for longest fingernails: 24 feet 7.8 inches. She hasn't cut them since 1979.

▶ The former Mrs. Marlyn Manson and most celebrated burlesque dancer in the world, Dita Von Teese, is the daughter of a manicurist.

▶ Kristina Preston was awarded $3.1 million dollars after she contracted herpes from a manicure at a salon that used nonsterile instruments in Aurora, Colorado.

▶ The ancient Turks are believed to be the first people to use a chemical hair process to remove unwanted hair. The concoction "rusma" combines yellow sulfide of arsenic, quicklime, and rose water.

three

THE TRAINER

Signs It's Time to Dump Your Trainer

▶ When he's spotting you, his cigarette ash falls on your face.

▶ He has a new workout plan—it's called helping him move.

▶ You go to the bathroom and he offers to spot you.

▶ He's so busy watching himself in the mirror that he trips over you.

▶ Every five minutes, he shouts "Nice game!" and slaps you on the ass.

Big Pain, No Gain

Within weeks of getting a place in Los Angeles, I received a special invitation in the mail from a local gym: a "Welcome to the Neighborhood" special membership offer. I showed up to meet the trainer for my one complimentary session. Their hope was that I'd love the trainer so much, I'd rush to sign up for more training sessions—but I knew better than to allow myself to get suckered into that kind of scam. I was a New Yorker, after all.

I checked in at the front desk, took a seat, and stared at all the perfect bodies working out. And when I say perfect, I mean zero body fat. The gym looked like something off the cover of *Fitness* magazine: rippled men lifting weights and flexing as perfectly sculpted women with little more than a washcloth covering their bits ran on treadmills. I started to feel anxious and intimidated, so much so I decided to bolt. I clicked my heels, pivoted, and smacked into Anthony, my assigned trainer who was standing in front of me, arm extended, ready to introduce himself. Anthony had a kind face and a gentle handshake. Realizing that I was about to bolt, he assured me that everything was going to be just fine, and I believed him.

It turned out that first day Anthony knew just how far to push me without making me resent him. He was present and engaged and didn't chat a lot, which is something I really value in a trainer. I need focus and dedication. He had a natural excitement about working out that inspired me. Within fifteen minutes, I found myself actually enjoying exercise: a first for me.

When my hour was up I felt as though I had lost five pounds and gained a foot in height. High from post-workout endorphins, I wanted one thing and one thing only: to have Anthony be my trainer. Noticing my excitement, Anthony magically whipped out a contract from his back pocket and placed it in front of me. "Yay,

Jodyne! Congratulations, girl. You did it. You're on your way! Now, if you'll just sign here, we can get started as soon as tomorrow." I ripped that pen out of his hand and scribbled my John Hancock without so much as reading a single line of the contract: so much for the jaded New Yorker.

A half-hour later, endorphin rush over, I looked at my contract and discovered that I had signed up for twenty training sessions with Anthony at zero discount. Usually, when you sign up for a series of prepaid workouts, you're offered some kind of discount off the price of a single workout—not me. There it was on the contract: the words "NO DISCOUNT." I made peace with my poor decision by convincing myself that Anthony was going to be worth every penny.

When I arrived for our next session, Anthony looked as if he were a million miles away. He was totally unfocused. My once present and engaged trainer was now more interested in his cell phone, texting his friends, and just about everyone at the gym that day except me, my abs, and my glutes. I was confused. This wasn't the same guy who had inspired me, gotten me excited about working out again; this was some tired, bored trainer who didn't want to be training any more. I prayed that he was having an off day—something we're all allowed once in awhile—so I let it slide. But I got the same Anthony the next session, and the session after that. Add to that the chatter: Anthony and his modeling contract, Anthony and his new hot girlfriend, Anthony and his struggle to change the part in his hair. I tried not to engage, hoping that he would talk less, but it didn't work. He was going through the motions, but with no excitement or interest. I was pretty good at counting my own reps, but the few times I lost count and asked him how many more I had to go, he answered with a question. "Four?"

Going to the gym became less and less exciting. I still had a number of pre-paid sessions to go with Anthony, but the idea of listening to his chatter made me tired and less willing to go to the gym. I stopped returning his calls, preventing him from setting up our next appointment. Since my contract was paid directly to the gym, Anthony only got his paycheck once I actually showed up—so he was actively putting in every effort to get me to do so. If only he had put an ounce of that energy into our workouts.

I asked the front desk to tell me Anthony's days off, and I only exercised when he wasn't there. That worked great until his schedule changed. One day, Anthony cornered me while I was on the treadmill. "Is everything okay?" he said.

"Sure, I'm sorry—I've just been super busy, that's all." It was a lie, but I wasn't about to dump him while on the treadmill. Not to mention that I was completely caught off guard.

"You sure about that? I noticed on the computer that you've only been coming in on my days off." Busted! I stopped my treadmill, took a deep breath and looked into his eyes. Here was my chance to tell him the truth, get it all out in the open. I could do this.

"Yep, I'm sure. No problem. No problem at all. We're good." I gently patted him on the shoulder and walked home. That was the last time I ever set foot in that gym.

What I Learned

The first time I joined a gym in New York, I asked the manager to match me with a trainer he thought would be right for me. He ended up pairing me with a dance-based trainer who couldn't have been a worse fit; he had me clapping and doing the grapevine. I still cringe just thinking about it, because if you know me at all, you know that I'm not a choreographed, cheerleader kind of girl. I was so turned off by Mr. Grapevine that I stopped going to the gym entirely. Obviously, I didn't do much better at the gym

I joined in Los Angeles, so after that experience I decided to stop wasting money and never join a gym again. I was done . . . until I researched this chapter and learned how important it is to be the one who takes control of my gym experience instead of handing it over to some random trainer most likely assigned by a gym manager who has his own agenda. After writing this chapter, I joined a new gym, interviewed three trainers, and went over my fitness goals with each, asking them about their individual workout styles and background. I made it clear that whomever I chose, I'd only commit to a few sessions before making up my mind. Interviewing them put me in the driver's seat.

I'm pleased to report that I found the right trainer for me. I'm constantly asking him questions, telling him to pay attention to me if I see his eyes wander. I let him get away with nothing. Come to think of it, I hope he's not thinking of dumping me.

Laying the Groundwork

▶ Be clear what you like and don't like about your trainer.

▶ If you haven't already, go over your fitness goals with him. Do you want to lose weight? Bulk up? Tone? Tell your trainer what you want and when you want it.

▶ Schedule check-ins every few weeks or once a month. Spend a few minutes reviewing your goals and fitness program, making sure that the two of you are on the same page. This is your opportunity to tell him what is and isn't working for you. It's also his heads-up that if things don't get better, you're going to be looking for a new trainer.

▶ Have another trainer lined up. Need help? Check out the National Strength and Conditioning Association at www.NCSA-lift.org

or www.AceFitness.org for a listing of certified personal trainers in your area.

Things Your Trainer Shouldn't Do

1. Push vitamins and supplements: Check with your doctor first.

2. Bully you into buying shakes, meal replacements, or other supplements sold at your gym: The markup is outrageous, and many gyms offer trainers a commission on whatever they sell.

3. Force you to do anything that doesn't feel right: Every body is different, and no body should be forced or manipulated into doing something that it's not comfortable doing.

4. Diagnose an injury: Your trainer might know more about your body than you do, but he's not a doctor. Leave the diagnoses to the professionals.

5. Think you're his therapist or best friend: If you find your trainer coming to you for advice or find yourself offering it, it's time to take a step back. Don't get caught taking care of your trainer.

How to Dump 'Em

NOT THE RIGHT FIT(NESS)

Not getting the results you hoped for? Feeling guilty about dumping your trainer? Chances are that if you lose the guilt, you'll shed the pounds. If you're eating a healthy diet, the only person who should feel guilty is your trainer; you're paying him good money so you can see a difference. The problem is many people are paired with the wrong trainer. Some trainers work best with clients who want to bulk up, while others get results with clients who want to lose weight. Some are trained in martial arts, others in sports. There are trainers who like to talk a lot, while others prefer to keep talking to a minimum. I spoke to a guy for this chapter whose gym manager matched him with a trainer who hurled insults at him in order to push him harder. The only thing it made him want to do was hurl on the trainer. Not every trainer is going to be the right fit, so it's your job to speak up.

STEPS

1. **Call your trainer or stop by the gym.**

2. **Start with a compliment or something positive.** *"I want to thank you for our past few workouts. You have a fast-paced and exciting workout style."*

3. **Tell him why you're dumping him.** *"However, I've decided I'd like to check out a few other trainers so that I can compare workout styles. It's important that I find the right match so I can maximize my results."* **For those of you who have become buddies with your trainer, try,** *"I think you're great and hope to continue hanging out with you outside of the gym, but I realize I've stopped pushing myself as hard since we've been hanging out. I need to start working out with another trainer, someone with whom I have less in common, so that I can get back on track. Thanks for understanding."*

4. **Allow him to respond. If he tells you that he can change his style to better suit you, say,** *"I appreciate that and will be sure to keep you in mind—however, my mind's made up."*

5. **Thank him.** *"Thanks for understanding."*

SCHEDULING CONFLICT

Looking for something a little less confrontational? Dump your trainer by finding out which days he has off, and then make an appointment with another trainer. If you like the new trainer better, let your old trainer know that your schedule has changed, and that the only day that now works for you is his day off. If he offers to come in on his day off, tell him, "I so appreciate the offer, but it turns out that I really connected with this other trainer, so I'm going to work with him for a while."

VIRTUAL FITNESS TRAINER

Save money by dumping your physical trainer in favor of a virtual one. Working out with a trainer online allows you to work out on your own schedule. With Web sites such as www.LiveHealthier.com, it's never been easier to design an individual program that suits your needs. Live Healthier offers individually tailored programs as well as unlimited, round-the-clock access to personal trainers, nurses, life coaches, registered dieticians, and physical therapists. Clients have the option of calling, chatting live, e-mailing, and videoconferencing. iPod users, check out www.PodFitness.com and download routines that make use of your own music. Even the Xbox 360 and the Nintendo Wii have fitness programs designed to get you fit.

WHAT YOU SAY: *"With my crazy schedule right now, I have to squeeze in my workouts at odd hours. A virtual trainer is my only alternative for the time being. Thanks for everything."*

BE PREPARED FOR HIM TO SAY: *"Those programs are awful. They don't show you what you're doing wrong."*

FINAL WORD: *"Luckily you've given me a strong foundation, so for the most part, I already know what I'm doing."*

DIRTY WORK

It's not a fun job, but somebody's got to do it—so why not let it be your gym's manager? Go to him and ask for a reassignment. Remember, it's his job to keep you coming back to the gym and buying more training sessions, so he will want to know why things didn't work out with your trainer. Ask him to tell your trainer that it was his idea to match you up with different person. Your next step is to not avoid seeing your old trainer at the gym. Make a point of smiling or waving hi to him. You don't have to have a conversation. If he confronts you and asks whether he did anything wrong, casually mention that you discussed it with the manager and the two of you decided that the new trainer would be a better match for you. It's not your responsibility to take care of your trainer's feelings, so if he wants to feel hurt, let him. This is about what's best for you, not your trainer.

OPPOSITES ATTRACT

Dump your trainer by telling him that you prefer working out with a trainer of the opposite sex—just make sure that you have another trainer lined up of the appropriate gender. Apologize and let him know that you didn't realize that you had a preference initially. My current trainer has put me on a few machines that have placed me in positions that—if I didn't feel completely comfortable with him—I would find totally embarrassing.

WHAT YOU SAY: *"I decided that I would feel more comfortable working out with a female trainer. It's nothing personal; I just realized there are a few machines that I'm not totally at ease with. Thanks for understanding."*

BE PREPARED FOR HIM TO SAY: *"Oh, please. I'm totally harmless, and in a relationship."*

FINAL WORD: *"I'm sure you are; this is just something I need to do for myself. Thanks again."*

In a Pinch

BIGGEST LOSER

Tell your trainer you've been chosen to be on a weight loss show. Let him know that you are going to be provided with a trainer for at least the next six months—and tell him how excited you are! You're going to be famous! Thank him for all his hard work and start singing the first few lines from "Hooray for Hollywood."

Q&A
Bob Harper
**LIFE COACH ON NBC'S *THE BIGGEST LOSER*
AND AUTHOR OF *ARE YOU READY!***

Q. *How do you tell your trainer that you're just not that into him?*
A. I would have to say that honesty is the best policy. Sometimes people don't fit, and personal training is so personal, so if you and your trainer are just not hitting it off, then no one will benefit and you will definitely not be getting the results that you are looking AND paying for. You should just sit him down and explain that this working relationship is not a "fit," and you will be moving on. Chances are he or she has already picked up on this feeling that you are having and is just waiting for you to make this move. Remember, you are not telling your soon to be ex-trainer that he has cancer, you are just telling him that you don't want to see him anymore—no biggie.

Q. *How do you know when your trainer's just not that into you?*
A. If your trainer is always late and walks in with an iced venti latte, he managed to get to Starbucks to get his drink knowing that he had an appointment with you—and just didn't care. If your trainer is texting during your session or taking incoming calls during your "set"; if he has no real plan or routine set up for your workout; if he is barely listening to you; and most of all, if he watches the clock and ends you a couple of minutes early and says, "You have been working so well today that I'm letting you go early"—yeah, right. He is just not that into you.

Q. *What questions should someone ask a trainer before deciding to work out with him?*

A. You would definitely want to look at some sort of résumé and a client list. I also would ask for referrals so you can do your own research. Make sure that the trainer that you are thinking about hiring is well versed in the type of body that you are striving to get.

Q. *What do you tell clients who are more concerned with letting you down than letting themselves down?*

A. You have to remind your clients that their session should ALWAYS be about their needs and what they are looking to achieve. I always say that I'm the messenger when I'm working with someone. Keep the light and direction on the client. It is about lifting them up, and not about the trainer's expectations.

Q. *What's the best way a person can ensure success in a training program?*

A. The best way to ensure success is to put in the time and effort. You have to realize that working with a trainer is not like going to the hair salon. When you go to a hair salon, you get immediate results—but with personal training, you must plant the seed and then water and feed that plant, and then eventually it begins to grow and you get to see the fruits of your labor—in time. Remember that you're doing a good thing for yourself for the long haul. There is no real quick fix.

Q. *What's the proper way to ask a trainer to keep his eyes on you—and not the hot body that just walked by?*

A. Well, we are all human, and unless you have more of a personal relationship with your trainer (which is a whole other question), there is no problem with him looking at a body he admires when one walks by. It is a whole other story if it interferes with your focus and your time that you are paying for. Your session should be ALL about you.

Q. *What are the most common mistakes trainers make with their clients?*
A. I think that the most common mistake is when they become friends with their clients. I have always found that, generally speaking, you should keep a professional distance with your clients and you save yourself the problem of friendly arguments and uncomfortable situations. Always keep in mind that this is the your profession, and you don't want to lose a client in the big picture.

Q. *What's the biggest mistake people make with their trainers?*
A. Same as above. A lot of times—and understandably so—you want to get close to your trainer because you spend a lot of time with them and they see you at your most vulnerable—warts and all. But remember, you are paying for a service and you should keep your distance, personally.

Q. *How do you ask a trainer to blab less and focus more?*
A. There is nothing worse than a trainer that goes on and on about what they did last night or what they are going to do on their weekend. You should nip it in the bud from the very beginning, and don't let it get out of hand—because if you do, it will be harder to have that conversation. But if you start from the very beginning by saying that you don't really want to have a lot of chitchat during your workout, the trainer should pick up on it and abide. However, if he doesn't really pick up that hint, just be straightforward and tell him. It really is no big deal, and he will be able to focus better on what he needs to do with you and, ultimately, what you are paying him to do.

Q. *Why do some guys wear jeans and boots to the gym?*

A. LOL!!! That is one that stumps even me. I have never understood why some guys do that. Maybe they think it is cool, but I don't get that at all. Living in Los Angeles for many years and working in gyms, I have seen that forever and it drives me crazy! It's right up there with wearing flip-flops at the gym! I hate it when I see that, too. You're in a gym to work out, not to be in your street clothes trying so hard to look like a badass. I recommend wearing workout gear in the gym with clothes meant for working out. Then, when it's time to go out, throw on your jeans and boots.

DumpipediA

▶ Madonna dumped her trainer, Carlos Leon, and then had a baby with him.

▶ According to American Sports Data, Inc., more than 6 million American adults use a personal trainer.

▶ Did you know that the training industry is unregulated and that anyone can call himself a trainer? Be sure and look for the letters "CPT" next to a trainer's name; this means that he is a certified personal trainer.

▶ What's the most popular month to sign up with a trainer?
    A. January
    B. April
    C. December

The answer is A. January. New Year's resolutions, anyone?

four

THE THERAPIST

Signs It's Time to Dump Your Therapist

▸ You spy a crossword puzzle on the clipboard where he's been taking notes.

▸ He tells you to stop crying.

▸ You tell him to stop crying.

▸ He takes personal calls during your session and you hear him say, "I can't talk now—in the middle of my session with koo-koo bear. Yeah. That's the one."

▸ He hands you a flyer inviting you to come and see him perform at the Improv.

We Need to Talk

When I first moved to Los Angeles, I decided to check out a therapist whom a very close friend had recommended. She warned me that Marcy practiced a unique style of therapy. I decided to proceed—largely because my friend had such amazing results with her.

The first time I approached her office, I was both nervous and excited. I spent the session telling her my life story and discussing the issues I wanted to work on during our time together. However, my session was cut abruptly short the minute that Marcy heard that I was in the entertainment business. She vaulted out of her La-Z-Boy chair, raced over to a box of cassette tapes, pulled one out, and popped it into her stereo. "Would you mind listening to this?" she said, nearly out of breath. "It's my son Frankie's voice-over demo reel. He's really talented, and I'd love to get some professional feedback." I reminded her that I was a just a writer and knew absolutely nothing about voice-overs, but it was too late; the cheesy instrumental music had started. For the next eleven minutes and twenty seconds I suffered through what sounded like Peter Brady in *The Brady Bunch* episode where he lost his voice the day before he and his siblings were supposed to appear on television and sing "Time to Change"—only there were no brothers and sisters helping Frankie out on his voice-over reel. Overcome, proud mother Marcy was jumping up and down on her couch like Tom Cruise on *Oprah*.

When the ordeal was over, Marcy looked at me and shouted, "Well? What do you think?" I lied, of course.

"Oh, he's great! What a voice." I said. Then instead of telling her how uncomfortable and inappropriate I found this, I started scribbling next week's appointment in my date book.

"She's just a little out there," said the friend who had introduced me to Marcy. "Stick with it. She's worth it."

To which I wanted to say, "You stick with it!" But since I was the master avoider, I kept going, too afraid to break up with her. In the following weeks—to Marcy's credit—I did learn how to effectively communicate with people in a way that doesn't blame or judge them, but I was incapable of practicing my new skills on her. Marcy continued to ignore my boundaries and I let it continue—until I reached my breaking point. One session, Marcy took the liberty of sharing with me private information about my friends who were still seeing her, discussing what their personal issues were and what her issues with them were. Done!

Over the next few days, I rehearsed what I was going to say. As I drove for my final appointment, my hands were sweating so much that they were sliding off the steering wheel. I knew what I had to do. I'd walk through that door of hers and immediately blurt out that I was done with therapy. Unfortunately, I walked into an empty room. Marcy was in the kitchen making some kind of wheat juice shake. She excitedly entered the room. "Oh, there you are. Good. So there's another client of mine—who just happens to be my favorite client—and I really think you guys would totally hit it off. You have so much in common. I gave him your number." I was speechless. She's fixing me up on a date? For real? And did she just refer to him as her favorite client? What was I, chopped liver? It's not that I wanted to be her favorite client, but it still hurt. My plan was aborted. Not only did I not break up with her, I went on the date.

Kevin was absolutely lovely, and she was right—we had tons of things in common. Unfortunately, because attraction is such a complicated thing, it just wasn't there for me. Now, in addition to having to dump Marcy, I also had to break her heart by telling her that her favorite client wasn't going to be running off to the altar anytime soon—at least not with me. The question was whether to break up with her first, or tell her about Kevin first; I chose Kevin, thinking it would be an easier transition. Boy, was I wrong. I walked in and found Marcy on the edge of her seat, with a giant grin on her face. Ugh. I took a deep breath, looked her straight in the eyes, and in the kindest way possible mentioned how amazing I thought Kevin was and how thrilled I was to have met him and that I hoped that we would be friends, but that it just wasn't there for me in a romantic way. The look on her face after I said that was frightening. The woman looked like she had a shiv in her hand and was about to stick it into me. She was devastated. Her face turned a shade of red that I had never seen before. She then opened her mouth and started yelling. "Well, I'd like to tell you something, Jodyne, and it's probably going to hurt." To which I put up my hand, hoping to stop her, but it was too late, the words were coming out of her mouth. "You're both sevens!" And there it was. My therapist had rated my attractiveness on a scale of one to ten.

I turned beet red. And to top it all off, I still couldn't dump her. I froze. But that didn't stop her from breaking up with me. Marcy was so pissed at me for rejecting Kevin that she dumped me on the spot, saying that she could no longer work with me.

What I Learned

I continued seeing Marcy long after I realized that she wasn't the right fit for me. If only I had spoken up and said something during our first session, the moment she jumped out of her seat and raced toward her stereo. But instead of saying something, I lost my voice. Writing this chapter taught me how important it is to trust your body and listen to what it has to say. I was terribly uncomfortable in that session, squirming around on the couch. This was my cue to speak up and say something. Mission failed—but lesson learned.

I spoke to a woman in Boston who was so afraid to dump her therapist that she started seeing a second one to help her break up with the first one. She spent thousands of dollars before waking up one day and realizing that she had forgotten why she was in therapy in the first place. A number of people continued seeing their therapists long after their issues were resolved because they were afraid of hurting their therapists' feelings. When asked if they knew how to terminate with a therapist, very few of them had any idea. I think this is one of the biggest mistakes therapists make with their clients—if they're trained in dealing with termination, how about giving the rest of us the benefit of their experience? After all, last I checked there were no guidebooks explaining how to leave a therapist. So the next time I go to a therapist, I'm going to ask him how he prefers to handle termination right from the get-go, before ever stepping a foot though his door.

Laying the Groundwork

▸ Write down your reasons for going to therapy in the first place and ask yourself if you've resolved those issues.

▸ Make a list of the reasons why you want to dump your therapist.

▸ Go over the list and make sure you're breaking up with him for the right reasons. For example, feeling scared and vulnerable is a normal experience in therapy, and usually signals the moments when we're most open to healing. If you've just shared a major life event with your therapist and your instinct is to flee, tell him. This could be the perfect opportunity to work through a major issue.

▶ Have check-ins. Discuss a time line and ask him how many more sessions he anticipates having with you. Just be sure you factor your willingness to work into the equation, since you have a great deal of control over whether any progress is made in your therapy.

▶ Ask your therapist how he prefers to handle termination. Do this as soon as possible, preferably before you're ready to dump him.

▶ Have another therapist lined up if you still need one. If you don't know where to go, check out www.PsychologyToday .com and www.GoodTherapy.org for more information about finding one in your area.

▶ Rehearse what you're going to say. Do you want to share your reasons with him, or do you prefer not to?

▶ Make it your priority to leave things on a good note.

Tip: Therapy should always be about your feelings. If you find that you're constantly taking care of him or are afraid of hurting him, it's time to dump him.

How to Dump 'Em

I STILL HAVEN'T FOUND WHAT I'M LOOKING FOR
Connecting with a therapist immediately is important no matter how highly he's been recommended—take it from me. I knew at the first session that my therapist wasn't right for me, but I continued to see her because my friend had had such success

with her. But everyone is different and what works for one person doesn't necessarily work for another. If you've gone to a therapist a handful of times and are not clicking with him, unless you want to keep wasting your money—dump him! Therapy is about tearing down walls, not hiding behind them. If you're not feeling a connection with him or the type of therapy he practices, it makes the process difficult—if not impossible.

WHAT YOU SAY: *"I'm sorry, but I was hoping for a stronger connection to this type of therapy. Since I didn't find it, I'm going to keep looking. Thank you for your time."*

BE PREPARED FOR HIM TO SAY: *"Perhaps we need to look at why you feel that way. It's natural to want to run. Let's explore your need to leave over the next few months."*

FINAL WORD: *"I'm sorry, this just isn't a fit for me. I need to trust my instincts."*

CALLING IT QUITS

When was the last time you heard of a therapist who turned to his patient and said, "Congratulations, you're done. Now go on, get out of here!"? I'm guessing the answer is never. This means it's up to you to tell your therapist when you're finished. Whatever issues come up surrounding termination, discuss them with your therapist. He's the best person with whom to work through them. Anxiety, abandonment, and rejection are all common feelings. Having feelings about leaving doesn't mean that you're not ready to stop going—it just means that issues that often come up when a significant relationship is coming to an end have been triggered. These are normal reactions.

Tip: Most therapists I spoke with suggested you give your

therapist at least two sessions to wrap everything up and allow proper closure.

1. **Start the session by telling your therapist that you wish to terminate.** *"After giving this careful consideration, I've decided I'm ready to terminate."*

2. **Announce when your last session will be.** *"Next week will be our last session."*

3. **Allow him to respond.** If he asks why you have decided to terminate, answer if you wish, but keep in mind that the decision is yours. If you really don't want to discuss your reasons, don't.

4. **If he asks you to reconsider, be firm.** *"I've made up my mind."* Sometimes a therapist might ask for additional sessions to finish working through an issue. Consider it carefully; you don't have to make up your mind that second. You can always say, *"I'll think about it, but unless I change my mind, next week will be my last session."*

5. **Thank him.**

CH-CH-CH-CHANGES

With so many types of therapy out there, it can be hard to know which one is right for you. Spend time and research other types of therapy. Then tell your therapist that you have decided to see someone who specializes in it.

WHAT YOU SAY: *"Thank you for all the work we've done together. Recently I've been reading about a type of therapy called EMDR (Eye Movement Desensitization Reprocessing) therapy.*

It's really been resonating with me, and so I've decided to check out a practitioner of that style of counseling. Today will be my last session."

BE PREPARED FOR HIM TO SAY: "Are you sure you're not trying to get out of doing the difficult work that we have started together? I think that if you stayed a little longer, we could really get to the bottom of this."

FINAL WORD: "While I appreciate your feedback, I've made up my mind."

LIFE COACH

Life coaches are part of a growing trend these days. Whereas traditional therapy focuses on healing emotional injuries from the past, life coaches focus on outcome by maximizing their clients' potential, both on a personal and on a career level. The International Coach Federation is the largest worldwide organization for business and personal coaching and claims to have more than thirteen thousand members worldwide. Check out its Web site at www.coachfederation.org and find a life coach.

WHAT YOU SAY: "Thank you so much for all your help. I've decided to put therapy on hold right now and start seeing a life couch."

BE PREPARED FOR HIM TO SAY: "Life coaches have no formal training. I think you should reconsider."

FINAL WORD: "I will keep that in mind, but for right now, this is what I've decided to do."

CASH POOR

Therapy isn't cheap, especially when your insurance isn't covering it. If money is an issue, dump your therapist by telling him that you need to cut back on your spending, starting with therapy. If he offers to reduce his rates or put you on a tab, politely decline.

Tip: Before choosing a therapist, call or sit down with a few different providers and discuss their styles so you know what you're comfortable with.

In a Pinch

I FOUND GOD!
Tell your therapist that you've had a recent spiritual awakening and have discovered the joys of a church or synagogue. This new way of life has given you all the inner peace and happiness you've ever wanted, so from now on your priest or rabbi will provide all the counseling you need.

Darlene Basch

**LICENSED CLINICAL SOCIAL WORKER AND
BODY PSYCHOTHERAPIST IN LOS ANGELES.**

Her Web site is www.TransformationTherapy.com.

Q. *Why is it so difficult for people to dump their therapists?*
A. Once people have developed a relationship with anyone, it's often hard to end it, especially with someone that could be considered an authority figure (such as a therapist). Many people put their therapists in a position of power and have a hard time doing what they think is best for themselves, especially if they feel that their therapist might protest or not agree with their decision. Childhood issues often play out with therapists. It's also common for people to treat their therapist like a parent and will therefore have a tough time acting independently if that was an issue in their childhood.

Q. *Why don't therapists discuss termination right from the get-go with their clients, making it easier for them when the time comes?*
A. If therapists discussed termination at the beginning, many people would have a difficult time feeling safe and comfortable, focusing instead on the end of the relationship. Generally, most therapists and clients do not know how long the relationship will last. Learning to tolerate the unknown and dealing with situations as they come up—such as termination—is often one of the benefits of therapy. Therapy gives clients the chance to put the changes they have made into practice. However, when a client comes in for something specific and short term, there can be discussion of how the decision is made to end therapy and how that would be done.

Q. *What's one of the biggest mistakes therapists make with their clients?*
A. One of the biggest mistakes therapists make is to become emotionally involved or attached to the outcome of what their clients do. In other words, while good therapists care about their clients, they have to maintain their boundaries so that their sense of well-being or sense of whether or not they are a good therapist is not based on what their clients decide to do with their lives. Therapists can guide clients by helping them understand themselves and showing them alternatives. Ultimately, clients are responsible for their lives, and their decisions are their own, not a reflection of the therapist.

Q. *What's a common mistake people make with their therapists?*
A. A common mistake people make with their therapist is to give the therapist responsibility for their lives. Many times clients come to therapists looking for the magic answers that will solve their problems and give the therapist too much power. Clients are responsible for the decisions they make and the way they run their lives. Therapists can offer guidance, different perceptions, and alternate approaches, but clients have the final decision on how to put this advice into action. Clients also make the mistake of doing what they think the therapist wants them to do instead of what feels right to them.

Q. *What advice can you offer someone who is afraid of hurting his therapist's feelings?*
A. It is not the client's responsibility to take care of their therapist's feelings. Clients are paying therapists for their service and therefore therapists are responsible for their own feelings. However, it is important to be respectful and considerate—as you would in any relationship. This means being honest about how you feel and giving advance notice when you are ready to leave.

Allowing time to process the end of the relationship is helpful for both parties. It is important to make sure that you like your therapist, understand the therapist's methodology, and are clear about expectations. To have a good working therapy relationship, it is essential that you take responsibility to speak up as soon as you feel things are not going in the right direction so you can avoid a bad breakup.

Q. *Can someone outgrow his therapist?*
A. Yes, people can outgrow their therapist. Each person begins therapy in a certain place. Over time, as you grow and change, it is possible to reach a point when you've learned all you can from your therapist and can benefit from a different technique or a new perspective.

Q. *What are the signs that it's time to dump your therapist?*
A. Sometimes clients feel that they have completed their therapy but don't know how to tell their therapists. Other times they become aware that their therapy is no longer helpful or productive, and they want to change therapists. There are also times when clients realize they do not really like their therapist, or their therapist has offended them in some way.

Q. *How should someone terminate with a therapist?*
A. Acknowledge to yourself that you're ready to break up with your therapist and be very clear about your reasons. Write in your journal about how you are feeling about doing this. Wait a day or two and review what you've written. Keep writing about this until you feel that you have expressed all your feelings, both positive and negative, about moving on.

Next, rehearse what you'll actually say to your therapist in your journal and/or with your friends. Then give notice by letting your therapist know a couple of sessions before you want to end the relationship that you're ready to quit. This will give you time to go through an ending process, in which you can review your progress and discuss your future goals. Be prepared to discuss your decision and process your feelings with your therapist. Your therapist may point out how your wanting to end therapy relates to issues you have been working on.

If you've gone through this process and are sure you're making the right decision to leave, even if your therapist does not agree, end the therapy at the time of your choosing.

Q. *Who is your favorite film/TV therapist?*
A. Judd Hirsch in *Ordinary People* does an outstanding job with a traumatized young man and his family, but my all-time favorite is Richard Dreyfuss in *What about Bob?* I thought that movie was hysterical.

DUMPIPEDIA

▶ Dr. Melfi dumped Tony Soprano on *The Sopranos* after she read a study that said therapy doesn't help sociopaths, it just enables them.

▶ According to www.FunFacts.com.au, Sigmund Freud was deathly afraid of the number sixty-two.

▶ The National Institute for Mental Health reports that anxiety disorders are the most common mental illness in the United States, affecting 40 million adults aged 18 and older—or 18.1 percent of the U.S. population.

▶ Laughter therapy is a type of therapy that uses humor and laughter to improve emotional well-being in order to facilitate improvement in health. It turns out our bodies' levels of neuroendocrine and stress-related hormones decrease during episodes of laughter.

▶ According to the National Institute for Mental Health, panic disorders affect 6 million people (2.7 percent of the population). Women are twice as likely to be affected as men.

part two
STICKY PEOPLE, STICKY SITUATIONS

THE NEIGHBOR

Signs It's Time to Dump Your Neighbor

▶ The number of stray cats he feeds grows by the hour.

▶ He's up on current events . . . after stealing your newspaper.

▶ He has Sunday drum circles in his front yard.

▶ He parks his motor home in front of your house and rents it out.

▶ He comes over every morning and asks to borrow an omelet—preferably one with mushrooms and cheese.

When You Don't Love Thy Neighbor

I live in an historic Hollywood 1930s chateau in Los Angeles where every apartment has character—original art deco tiles, lighting fixtures, and crown molding. The major disadvantage is that the walls are paper-thin. Initially it wasn't much of an issue because I had quiet neighbors, all of whom looked out for one another without stepping over any personal boundaries. But then one day my lovely next-door neighbor moved out and in came Sharon, a young college "student." I put "student" in quotation marks because she was, in reality, anything but—when I asked her what school she went to, she stared intensely at me for twenty seconds before saying, "Oh, uhm, school? CU?" She answered my question with a question.

"California University?" I asking, knowing it was the fictitious university in the television show *Beverly Hills 90210*.

"Yes!" she said with great relief and walked away wearing her signature outfit: white short-shorts, silver heels, and a super tight tank top. The color of the tank may have changed, but the outfit always stayed the same—even in winter.

From the minute Sharon moved in, there was a steady stream of noise coming from her apartment. My bedroom window that I loved to keep open for fresh air now had to be closed at all times to escape her constant chatter. In a short period of time, I heard about her love of Wet n' Wild nail polish as well as whether or not she thought unicorns existed; she went back and forth on that one for some time. Sharon was also obsessed with working out, something she loved to do with her front door wide open, claiming it was for air—but if anyone wanted to watch, that was fine, too. She divided her workouts between her Suzanne Somers's Thighmaster and her hot pink rebounding machine. And she had a well-choreographed dance routine to Oxo's "Whirly Girl," performed on her trampoline, hands wildly clapping and knees bouncing high.

Sharon also had a peculiar way of answering every question with, "Well, I'm from Lancaster," as though that would somehow qualify whatever she was about to say. For those of you that don't know Lancaster, it's about an hour north of Los Angeles and is one of the major crystal meth capitals of the world. If I asked her to please close her front door, she'd respond with, "Sorry, I'm from Lancaster!"

Problems escalated when Sharon started going out late into the morning hours, something her dog didn't enjoy and let the entire neighborhood know this by howling all night. And by all night, I mean *all* night. People yelled profanities out their windows to get the dog to shut up, but he refused. My neighbors and I all left notes on her door, but Sharon would shrug them off and make some comment about Lancaster. There didn't seem to be any part of Sharon able to register that none of us could get a wink of sleep at night. Nor did she get the message when the next-door neighbors started throwing eggs at her window, which always managed to hit my adjoining window. She complained about school running late, but I never once saw a textbook in her hands or a backpack on her shoulders. I tried offering nicely to walk her dog if she was going to be in "class" late, but she said it wouldn't be necessary.

My next step was getting the building to sign a petition asking her to keep her dog quiet. I was hoping my landlord would do something with it, but when I handed it to him he refused to take it from my hand, letting it fall instead on the ground. I decided to leave it under Sharon's door, hoping she would take it seriously. She didn't.

The cops took it a little more seriously when we called to report the noise, and they began showing up at Sharon's door at all hours of the night. A week later, the local humane society arrived with my landlord and rescued Sharon's dog. Sharon cried for days. I tried to be as sympathetic as I could, but it's hard to show compassion when you're operating on three hours of sleep a night.

A few days later, I came home as Sharon was putting the last of her boxes into a U-Haul truck. "I'm going back to Lancaster," she said. When I asked her about school, she looked at me blankly and said, "What school? I'm a stripper. I can do that anywhere. But at least in Lancaster the people don't throw eggs at your window and steal your dog!" Then she slammed the door shut and headed north.

What I Learned

Over the years, I've had the misfortune of living next to two college girls who blasted Pat Benatar at all hours of the night, an upstairs neighbor who lifted weights at 6 a.m., dropping them and jolting me from sleep, and a drunken downstairs neighbor who shouted karaoke 'till dawn. Sure, I complained to anyone who would listen—friends, family, my empty bedroom—but heaven forbid I should actually pick up a phone or knock on a door. There was just no way I could do it.

What I learned while writing this chapter is how important it is to give your neighbor the benefit of the doubt. We all have different ideas of how much noise is acceptable, and the only way we can come to a mutually agreeable limit is by addressing the issue in person, something I never did with Sharon. Assuming that your neighbor will magically know he's being too loud is unrealistic. Most likely Sharon felt ganged up on. I never tried talking to her in person, explaining how the dog kept me up or that I could hear her conversations word for word when her window was open. A personal connection can make a world of difference. Does this mean I'm going start knocking every time a neighbor blasts his TV? Probably not, but I'll take baby steps, like mentioning it when I see him in the hallway. At least now I know that there are city laws that cover the specifics of what the legal noise levels are. On second thought, maybe I am ready to knock on my neighbor's door. The journey down the hall begins with but a single step.

Laying the Groundwork

▶ Situations with neighbors don't go away until you take action.

▶ Consider the possibility that your neighbor doesn't know there's a problem.

▶ Don't assume that your view is right and your neighbor's is wrong. There are always two sides to every issue, so be open-minded.

▶ Write down your problems and come up with possible solutions.

▶ Commit to working things out as neighbors first, before involving other people.

▶ If you live in an apartment, alert your landlord to the situation as soon as possible. Most leases have a clause that deals with neighbors and noise violations. If he refuses to help, you can take your landlord to small claims court for maintaining a nuisance on the property. Chances are, he will step up as soon as you mention court.

▶ Don't seek revenge against your neighbor. As tempting as it may sound, it's likely to make things worse.

▶ Research local laws and ordinances. You can look them up at city hall or your local public library.

How to Dump 'Em

KNOCK KNOCK

While you may not be able to comprehend the logic behind moving heavy furniture at 3 a.m. or singing Anne Murray's greatest hits 'till dawn, remember that there's a chance your neighbor has no idea you can hear him. Knock on his door and tell him, but know that if you go in attacking, you'll most likely be met with a neighbor who won't like you very much. So be considerate.

Tip #1: One of the biggest mistakes people make regarding their neighbors is involving a third party. It's harder for your neighbors to continue negative behavior once they've made a personal connection with you. Speaking to them directly sends the message that you hope to work things out amicably—but the minute you involve a third party, you take the friendly factor off the table, putting your neighbors on the defensive.

Tip #2: Be aware of your tone. There's a right way to say something and a wrong way. Make sure you know the difference. This is not the time to judge him. If he's leaving junk in his yard, for instance, don't bring his character into question by calling him untidy. Also, you're not there to blame him—you're there to come to a mutual understanding—so stay calm.

STEPS

1. **Knock on his door. Give the impression that you want to work this out together.** *"Sorry to bother you—I'm sure*

you're not aware, but the walls in this building are paper-thin. I hear almost everything."

2. **Offer a solution or compromise.** *"How would you feel if we set some quiet hours we can both agree to? I don't mind if your son wants to practice his drums after school, but on the weekends, before 9 a.m., is tough."* Suggest, but don't demand.

3. **Let him respond.**

4. **Acknowledge his feelings even if you don't understand or feel the same way. It demonstrates that you care.**

5. **Give him your phone number and thank him.** A little appreciation goes a long way. *"Thank you so much for being willing to work things out."*

DEAR NEIGHBOR

If you've had a hard time connecting with your neighbor in person or by phone, write him a letter using the same ideas discussed above. Define the problem, offer solutions, and thank him. The intent of the letter is not to threaten him; it's to gently ask him to pay attention to your concern.

WHAT YOU CAN WRITE: *"Hi _____. I tried stopping by the other day to discuss the trees that were planted in your yard recently. It appears that some of them are actually on my property. I'd like to discuss the situation with you so that we can come up with a solution together. Thanks for your cooperation."*

Tip: Be sure to keep a copy of all correspondence between yourself and your neighbors just in case you need it as evidence in the future, should your issue go to court or involve the police.

CALLING ALL COPS

If your neighbors are keeping you up all night with their loud parties and music and you've tried calling them and knocking on their door, call the cops. Excessive noise is often a criminal misdemeanor violation. I once had a next-door neighbor who played club music from 2–4 a.m. I left him notes, but he ignored them. Finally, I called the cops. Guess what? I never heard his music again. Turns out that he had had problems with the law in the past, and the last thing he wanted was a cop showing up at his front door. Problem solved.

Tip: For those of you who are having issues with a barking dog, call animal control at once and they'll send someone out to your neighbor's house or apartment.

THE MEDIATOR

In more complicated situations—such as those dealing with fences and trees—consider calling a mediator, especially if the two of you are unable to come to a compromise. Mediators are trained to listen to both sides of a dispute and objectively offer a resolution. There are over five hundred neighborhood mediation centers around the nation that specialize in resolving bitter battles between neighbors—depending on where you live, you may even be able to find one for free or a token fee. Mediators have a 90 percent success rate. Find one by looking up "mediators" in the Yellow Pages, going on the American Arbitration Web site at www.adr.org, or calling your local courthouse.

PEOPLE'S COURT

If you've tried everything and your issue still isn't resolved, consider taking your neighbor to court; having a neighbor you can't get along with is a serious problem. Going to court gives you the opportunity to ask for money and/or a judge's order making your neighbor responsible for his violations.

Evidence to Bring with You to Court

1. Copies of the laws your neighbor is violating.

2. Documentation of contact you've had with your neighbor to discuss the situation: phone records, copies of letters, notes left on door.

3. Journal of times and dates when you've recorded the problem.

4. Police records.

5. Letters or petitions from neighbors.

In a Pinch

MY HUSBAND/WIFE IS A MANIAC!

Put on your actor's hat and go knock on your neighbor's door. When he answers, introduce yourself and tell him about your spouse, the sleepwalker. Let him know that you felt obligated to give him a heads-up that when your spouse hears loud noises at night, he is out the door in no time with a baseball bat in hand. Nothing's ever happened, but you just feel more secure when everyone in the neighborhood knows about his little excursions. Then thank him and head home.

NOSEY NELLY

For those of you with a nosey neighbor who is constantly snooping or who talks endlessly while you struggle with heavy bags, start speaking gibberish to him. You'll know when you've done a good job by the look on his face.

Dumpipedia

▶ Neighbors of Mary-Kate and Ashley Olsen are desperately trying to dump them from their West Village neighborhood, claiming that the sisters are "disruptive, intrusive, and totally disrespectful."

▶ RottenNeighbor.com is a real estate search engine that helps you find out about bothersome neighbors before signing a lease or buying a home. Members can post memos about annoying neighbors and get advice from others.

▶ The Hatfield-McCoy feud was rumored to have begun in 1873 when a pig owned by Randolph McCoy crossed over into Floyd Hatfield's land, who then claimed ownership of the animal, saying that it was on his property. Fast forward to 1979, when both families agreed to tape an episode of *Family Feud* in which they played for a cash prize and a pig. The McCoys won.

▶ Arlene and Willis Hatch of Alto, Michigan, left their neighbors nearly $3 million when they died.

▶ The Good Neighbor Policy was established by Franklin D. Roosevelt in 1933 as a way to improve relations between the United States and
    A. Latin America
    B. Russia
    C. China
    D. Canada

The answer is A. Latin America.

six

THE HOUSEGUEST

Signs It's Time to Dump Your Houseguest

▶ She shows up in a U-Haul truck.

▶ She complains that there isn't a mint on her pillow.

▶ She arranges for her mail to be forwarded to your address.

▶ She hands you a list of things she wants from the market.

▶ She brings her cats with her—all ten of them.

Mi Casa Is Not Su Casa

I'll never forget my very first apartment without roommates. The location was perfect, right on the border of Soho and the West Village in Manhattan. Granted, it was tiny and a steep fourth-floor walkup, but it was mine: the dirt, the filth, the color of the walls, all mine. I barely managed three days on my own before my first houseguest arrived. Apparently having an apartment in a desirable location is very attractive to, well, everyone. Before I knew it friends were crawling out of the woodwork, some of whom I hadn't seen in over ten years. Guess who was suddenly their best friend? It didn't seem to matter that I couldn't remember some of their last names.

One such houseguest was my freshman roommate, Shelly. We had lost touch after graduation when she moved away. She was looking to make a move back to the city so she could pursue her musical career and needed a place to crash while looking for an apartment, just for "a week or two, tops. I've been speaking to record people and should be signing a contract within the next week or so." Not one to turn away a friend in need, I took her in.

That "week" quickly grew into a month, and Shelly was making herself more and more at home: my home. She even started redecorating my apartment—replacing my curtains with her own, taking down my family photographs and replacing them with a batik hanging from an old Grateful Dead concert. As the days went on my apartment was becoming less and less my aesthetic and more and more her own. When I would ask how her search for an apartment was going, she always had some excuse for why she needed another night on my couch—from spraining her finger to having low blood sugar—you name it, chances are she used it.

Until I hit my breaking point. I was coming home from a long day at work, exhaustedly climbing my steep stairs, ready to kick off my shoes and relax in front of the tube—preferably alone. When I reached the top I was beyond amazed to see the old college sock wrapped around my doorknob. Now, that may have worked in school as a signal that she was "getting busy" with someone inside and to tell me that I needed to find someplace else to sleep, but it wasn't going to fly that night. I knocked loudly on the door. Five minutes later, some half-naked guy was scurrying out my front door.

The following day, we had the talk. It didn't exactly go as I had planned. She interpreted my gentle words of encouragement to spread her wings and fly as me abandoning her and crushing her musical dreams. Buckets of tears came next, and she begged me for one more week, which I reluctantly gave her, but by this point, my respect for her had dwindled. When the week ended and she was still there, I had nothing but ill feelings toward her. I felt taken advantage of, and—in a less than healthy moment—I took her curtains and Grateful Dead hanging down, packed up all her belongings, and left her a note that read, "Please be gone by the time I get home." I never saw her again.

What I Learned

I've always been a sucker when it comes to having houseguests. I say yes when I don't really want to and end up resenting my guests when they've overstayed their welcome. I know; it's not very nice of me. What I learned while writing this chapter is the importance of taking responsibility for your actions regarding houseguests. Saying yes without knowing how long they are planning on staying is *my* mistake, not theirs. When I think back to Shelly, I now see that I should have been much clearer with her about exactly how long she'd be able to stay. I wish that I had told her that two weeks was my limit: nothing personal. Because I never spoke up, there's a chance that she had no idea that she had outstayed her welcome. This is why from this day forward I am going to come up with an exact number of days that I'm comfortable having someone stay with me ahead of time. I will share that number with the next person who calls me up asking to crash on my couch for a month. There's a fine line between a houseguest and a house pest. By presenting my well-thought-out number ahead of time, the line will hopefully never be crossed again.

Laying the Groundwork

▶ Write a list of reasons why you want to dump your houseguest.

▶ Ask yourself if you've been clear about what you expect her to do while she is staying with you. For instance, do you want her to do her own dishes, laundry, or driving? If you haven't already made this clear, do so now.

▶ Warn her. Remind her of what you asked her to do while staying with you. Let her know that if she doesn't toe the line, you're going to ask her to leave.

▶ Rehearse what you're going to say to your houseguest. Decide what outcome you're hoping for. When do you want her to leave? Tonight? Tomorrow? Do you want to remain friends with her or never see her again?

▶ Get back all your personal items still in her possession: keys, clothes, GPS, garage door openers, etc.

How to Dump 'Em

WE NEED TO TALK

Friend, friend of a friend, or relative, you let this person come into your home—therefore it's up to you to take responsibility for the situation. While you stew, totally amazed by the thoughtlessness of your houseguest, consider that there's a good chance that she's thinking that you actually enjoy having her around. If you can't muster up the courage to tell her to leave, remember that it's all in how you say it; if you think it's going to be uncomfortable, it will be. If you're concerned with being labeled a bad host, take a step back and realize that she is the one who has overstayed her welcome. Stop caring about what she thinks of you and start thinking about what other people are going to say once they hear what a pushover you are.

STEPS

1. **Pick a time to sit down with her when you know she doesn't have plans.**

2. **Gently ask her to give you an exact day of departure. Try, *"I want to check in with you about the exact day you plan on leaving so that I know when I can get back to my normal routine."***

3. **Allow her to respond. If she tells you to do what you need to do and not worry about her, don't back down! Try, *"I'll keep that in mind, but you still haven't answered my question. What day are you leaving?"* If she tells you that she hasn't decided yet, help her out. *"How does Wednesday work for you?"***

4. **If you're still met with resistance, be firm. You've already given her an inch—she has taken a mile. If you decide to allow her to stay longer, that's okay. Just don't end the conversation without a concrete date of departure.**

5. **Confirm the date that she will be leaving and, if appropriate, ask her if there's anything else you can do to help her leave on that day. For example:** *"Great. Wednesday it is. Let me know if I can drive you to the train station."*

OUT WITH THE OLD, IN WITH THE NEW

If your houseguest still isn't getting the message, invent another houseguest. Tell her the time and date of the fictitious newcomer's arrival. Don't say in a few days; say, "She's arriving on Monday at 9 a.m." For those in need of a little extra help, mention a crisis or medical condition that your new guest is going through, and how important it is for you to really give her some quality one-on-one time. "Did I tell you that Debbie is going through a divorce? Terrible!" If your houseguest has the nerve to ask for an extension, apologize and say, "I'm sorry, I really need this alone time with my friend, whom I haven't seen in years."

CHOOSING CHORES

There's nothing worse than a houseguest who starts barking orders and demanding meals, or the ones who just sit there expecting you to wait on them hand and foot. I once had friends in town from Europe and they did nothing but sit on my couch. They waited for me to get up in the morning so that I could cook them breakfast and drive them around. Their excuse was that they didn't understand American appliances or driving in Los Angeles. Oh, really? They don't have toasters in France? This is why you have to give your houseguests an incentive to leave; do this by jotting down chores for them. Grocery shopping, laundry, unloading the dishwasher, and walking the dog are all acceptable. Keep in mind that the bigger the task, the quicker the exit. I gave this piece of advice to my friend Josh who had an old fraternity brother staying with him for a few nights. When the few days were up, there were no signs that this guy was going anywhere anytime soon. Josh went home that night and told his pal that he'd better get a good night's rest, because the next day they were going to be painting the house and building a tool shed in the backyard. Guess what? He was gone by the time Josh got up.

In a Pinch

"I DON'T FEEL SO GOOD"

This option requires basic acting skills; if you're a little rusty, try it out first with a friend or the nearest mirror. The "I don't feel so good" routine requires you to pretend that you're about to vomit on your guest. Unbutton your shirt, mess with your hair, and put on your best sick face—maybe even moan a little. Give your guest a look that suggests that you are seconds from tossing on her. It helps to regurgitate a bit before racing to the nearest bathroom and slamming the door. Throw her a garbled, "I need to be alone" from behind the closed door. And if you're really up for a challenge, pretend to actually throw up.

"LOOK! A GHOST!"

Want to spook your houseguest right out of your home? Tell her that you've got a family of ghosts hanging around the house. Most of them are gentle, but there is one that's a little mean, and you just want her to be prepared—especially around sharp instruments. Then stare just slightly past her, telling her not to move—but that there's a spook directly behind her. Then start running!

NO AIR CONDITIONING AGAIN!

For those of you who live in areas with hot temperatures and high humidity—a place where air conditioning is a must—shut all the windows in your home and tell your houseguest that your air conditioner is out of commission. Tell her that the last time this happened, it took a week before you could get the air conditioner up and running again. She should be out your door within minutes.

AMERICA'S MOST WANTED

Dial 1-800-CRIME-TV from the nearest phone and let *America's Most Wanted* know that you have a houseguest who resembles one of the criminals on their television show; that should do the trick.

Q&A
Kato Kaelin
HOST AND ACTOR

Q. *What's the best way to ask a houseguest whether he ordered porn?*
A. I would suggest start by hinting around. Like, "Do you know what Spankvision is?" Drop a few of these types of comments and if they don't confess, present them with the bill and flat out ask them if they ordered it.

Q. *How do you get reimbursed if he did?*
A. Ask for the money. Then ask why you weren't invited.

Q. *How many days can a houseguest stay before you should ask him to pay rent?*
A. One month. But make sure and assign them chores after two weeks: the longer the stay, the bigger the task.

Q. *Is it okay for a houseguest to sunbathe naked by the pool?*
A. Only if he brings the Hawaiian Tropic bikini contest with him.

Q. *Do you think it's okay for a houseguest to break something, then crazy glue it back together?*
A. If the houseguest is me, then absolutely! Otherwise the answer is yes, as long as you have a good excuse to cover your ass (like, say, an earthquake).

Q. *Have you ever stolen anything as a houseguest?*
A. No, but I did just recently give Larry King my copy of O.J.'s house key.

Q. *How do you know whether your houseguest is going to testify against you in court?*

A. If they suddenly get a better offer and move into the guesthouse of the prosecutor, you're in trouble.

Q. *Is it possible to dump a houseguest and save the friendship?*

A. Absolutely. Sit them down and use reverse psychology on them. Tell your houseguest that you're doing them a favor. Be direct and explain that it's time for them to go. And do it with a smile on your face—always with a smile.

Q. *If you were reincarnated and came back as a houseguest, whose house would you chose to live in and why?*

A. My own, because I'm the only one dumb enough to actually live in a house behind my own home.

Q. *If you were an animal, what animal would it be and why?*

A. A termite. This way if I can't live in a house, I will at least be able to eat it.

Q. *The whole O.J. thing aside, what's the worst thing that has happened to you as a houseguest?*

A. That was my first and only time as a houseguest: Let's face it, there's nothing worse than a double homicide.

DUMPIPEDIA

▶ Early in his career, Gene Hackman hosted Dustin Hoffman as a houseguest in his one-bedroom apartment in New York City. Hoffman was only supposed to stay a few nights, but rumor has it he wouldn't leave. Instead of dumping him, Hackman took him around town to look for his own place.

▶ *Houseguest* was a 1995 feature film starring Sinbad and Phil Hartman.

▶ The queen of etiquette, Peggy Post, wrote on GoodHouse keeping.com that houseguests should thank their hosts by bringing a small gift, such as a bottle of wine.

▶ "Houseguest" is the name of a rock band from Akron, Ohio. The San Francisco–based literary magazine *McSweeney's* called them "the best pop band in America."

▶ According to the BBC's *Good Homes* magazine, smoking is considered the worst houseguest behavior. This is followed by overstaying one's welcome and criticizing home decoration.

seven

YOUR KID'S FRIEND'S PARENTS

Signs It's Time to Dump Your Kid's Friend's Parents

▶ They bring their own sleeping bags in addition to their children's when your kids have a sleepover party at your house.

▶ They conveniently show up at your house at dinner time to get their kids.

▶ Every time you're at their house, they try to convert you to their religion.

▶ Whenever you see them, they try to convince you to buy a time-share with them in Granada.

▶ They invite you to their house for a swingers' party.

Not Meeting the Parents

My sister Susan is one of the kindest people I know. Because she is so open, everyone wants to talk to her: the cashier at Whole Foods, the teller at the bank, the guy at the toll booth, and the mother of her daughter's new friend, Janet. Janet complained about everything, from her gym membership at Curves to the high price of gas to the color of an M&M. You name it, she griped about it.

Since part of being a parent is arranging play dates with your children's friends, it didn't take long before Janet was calling Susan to arrange one. Susan knew what that meant: more complaining. The first play date was to take place at Susan's home from 1 to 5 p.m. on Sunday. In order not to open herself up to Janet, Susan came up with a game plan. Janet would drop her son Jacob off at 1 p.m., leave, and Susan would let the kids play while she caught up on her mounds of paperwork. Perfect. But nothing's ever really perfect, and Susan's plan was not Janet-proof. Instead of dropping Jacob off and leaving the way other parents did, she took a seat at Susan's kitchen table and made herself comfortable. When Susan tried to excuse herself to get back to her paperwork, Janet responded with a remark about there never being enough time in the day to get everything done. She then spent the next four hours exhausting my poor sister with more complaining.

Susan tried her best to politely tap her watch and stare at the clock at 5 p.m., but Janet was just not getting the hint that it was time for her to leave, so Susan got up to make her family dinner. Janet watched as Susan sliced and diced vegetables, washed lettuce, and took out the tofu. And then what Susan was hoping to avoid happened; Janet said, "Hmmm. That smells amazing, what are you making?" Susan wasn't sure what she was referring to, since she hadn't started cooking and raw vegetables don't have much of a smell.

"Tofu vegetable stir fry," said a tired Susan.

"Oh, that's my favorite!" said Janet. Later we discovered that when Janet was hungry, everything was her favorite: meatloaf, pizza, raisins, all her favorites.

"Well. Um, would you and Jacob like to stay?" said Susan reluctantly.

"Only if you want us to!" said Janet. Susan couldn't help but feel tricked.

And that was just the beginning. Soon, Janet was showing up whenever she pleased, sometimes without Jacob. Knowing that Susan never locked her back door, Janet would show up and, if no one was home, she would just take a seat at the kitchen table and wait. When she wasn't waiting, she was ringing Susan on the telephone, always under the guise of making a play date for the kids—but really just to complain. We all begged my sister to say something, but Susan was never good at saying no—unless she's high on pain medication.

New England winters are a bitch, and Susan fell victim to the bitch when she was taking a stroller out of her minivan after a snowstorm. She didn't realize that she was standing on black ice. Just as she had the weight of the stroller in her hands, her feet came out from under her, dropping her flat on her back, stroller on her stomach. The doctor said that she had tweaked her back and put her on medication to ease the pain—but those pills also eased her inhibitions. Suddenly my sweet sister became sassy, telling people exactly what she was thinking—no holds barred.

During the next play date, Janet took her seat at Susan's table, picked up a soup spoon, and, because she simply could not stop herself, launched into a complaint about the size of a soup spoon. Janet felt that if a spoon was specifically designed to eat soup, it should be designed differently, allowing for an easier transition of broth into one's mouth. This was my sister's breaking point. She cut Janet off and launched into her own complaint—about

Janet. "You know you're not supposed to just stay here when the kids have a play date. It's for the kids. If I wanted you to stay, I would have asked you to. And last I checked, I hadn't asked—not once." And with that, Janet got up from the table and left. Unfortunately, she left without her son, whom she sheepishly crept back for five minutes later.

By the time that Susan's back had healed and she had run out of narcotics, she had a number of apologies to make—but it was Janet she felt the worst about. It was true that she had wanted to dump her for months, but this was not the way she had envisioned doing it. And the last thing she wanted was for it to affect her daughter's relationship with Jacob—so her first apology was to Janet, who accepted, and was about to launch into how dangerous painkillers are—but stopped herself. There would be no more complaining. The play dates continued, with Janet dropping Jacob off outside and beeping her horn to signal that she was there to pick him up. And that was just fine with Susan.

What I Learned

Just because your children get along doesn't mean that you're automatically going to get along with the parents. There's nothing I dread more than having to feign interest in someone; I'm terrible at it. I sigh a lot, my shoulders start twitching, and my eyes refuse to stay focused. But part of being a parent is talking to other parents, and that means having to be polite. For years, I've watched my sister engage in conversations with people I know she can't stand. It's scary how good she is at it—so good, in fact, that it makes me wonder how many times she's feigned interest in me.

I spoke to a lot of parents for this chapter. All of them at some point had either broken up with or wanted to break up with the parent of one of their children's friends. Most of them mentioned that they've known multiple parents whom they've wanted to dump. I learned that the most important thing to do is to constantly show how busy you are. This means telling the other parent about your plans while your children are playing so she doesn't assume that you have all the time in the world for her. You also have to be clear that play dates are for kids and not parents. Parents who were able to dump other parents said that you have to assume nothing. You have to spell out everything, grabbing the bull by the horns and establishing clear boundaries right from the get-go. This is something my sister was not able to do with Janet. Make sure that nothing is vague, from drop-off times to pick-up times. Give the parent the impression that you are scheduling appointments, not arranging a social gathering. Next!

Laying the Groundwork

▶ Ask yourself how dumping your kid's friend's parents is going to affect your child.

▶ Write a list of the things you don't like about your kid's friend's parents.

▶ Look at the list and decide whether you might be unfairly judging them. See if there's anything you can do differently in order to get along better.

▶ Start disengaging from the parents as much as possible.

▶ Set boundaries. Let the parents know what you're willing and unwilling to do regarding play dates. For example, if you're hosting a sleepover pizza party and the parents tell you that their child doesn't eat pizza and instead suggest a four-course meal for you to make from scratch, tell them, "I'm sorry, that's not possible—but if you want to prepare something for your child ahead of time, I'd be happy to serve it with the pizza." So set those boundaries and honor them. As soon as you start making exceptions, you give the impression you're willing to accommodate anything.

How to Dump 'Em

NO TIME LEFT FOR YOU

For those of you dealing with a parent who wants you to be her new best friend, nip things in the bud the minute a date has been set in motion. As soon as she asks you to get together, take control of the conversation by making it crystal clear you're busy and have no time to hang out with her.

PARENT #1: *"We should really make a plan for our kids to get together soon."*

YOU: *"That would be great! I'll be home all weekend, building shelves and shellacking them. Why don't you drop Jimmy off at 1 p.m. and the two kids can play for a few hours while I try and get some work done. We eat at 6 p.m., so if you want to come back at 5 p.m. to pick up little Jimmy, that would be great."*

In this situation, you've taken control by suggesting that the play date be at your house at a specific time, and you've used the words "drop off," making it clear that she shouldn't expect cake and coffee or plant herself at your kitchen table and chat for a few hours while your kids play. You've also mentioned that you have a project that needs your full attention, getting the point across that you have no time for her. The more you learn to take control of the conversation and tell other parents what you want to have happen, the easier it will get. It just takes practice.

If the parent wants to get together as a foursome, try blaming your spouse's busy schedule. Let her know that your partner is so busy that you never get to see him anymore. Then mention how excited you are to have date night this weekend, or whatever night the other couple wants to get together.

For those of you dealing with parents who have big personalities, and who refuse to allow you to take control of the conversation, that's okay—tell them that you need to check your schedule and get back to them. This allows you time to collect your thoughts and come up with plan B—which is to change the plan so that it accommodates you.

PARENT #2: *"Let's take the kids to the play gym on Sunday. We're painting the guest bathroom and I have no idea what color to use. I'll bring swatches and show you. I'll pick you up at 10 a.m."*

YOU: *"I'm going to need to call you back about Sunday, because I have to check my calendar."*

YOU (CALLING HER BACK): *"I promised _____ that I would do _____ on Sunday. I'd love it if you would take the kids to the gym. You can even drop off the swatches, and I would be happy to look at them while you're out."*

If the parent wants to come in and socialize, do not sit down with her. Stay standing. Assume that she forgot you have plans and remind her.

PARENT #2 (SEATED): *"So, how are things? What's new?"*

YOU (STANDING): *"I'd love to chat, but I'm in the middle of_____.
Thanks so much for taking the kids."*

Tip: If the parent looks hurt, I like to pay a compliment; say something nice either about the shirt she's wearing or about her child. I find that it changes the mood and makes for an easier exit.

And finally, for those parents who have kids who require them to wait a few minutes in order to settle in, tell them to take their time, and that you'll be in the other room if they need you—otherwise, you'll see them in a few hours when the play date's over. It's all about directing and controlling the plans and conversations. Once this becomes habit, you'll be amazed to discover how much stress you've eliminated from your life.

DO NOT ENTER

For those of you like my sister who can't find a way to get your kid's friend's parents to leave your house, implement the "do not enter" policy. This means you do whatever it takes to not allow them inside your house: their kids, yes, but the parents? No way. If the play date is at your house, run outside the minute you hear their car pull up, making sure the parents do not get out of the car. It's easier if you can arrange play dates at their house or another location. If their child comes home with yours after school, offer to drive her home. If they attempt to ambush you at their house, excuse yourself politely by letting them know that you need to be somewhere else and are running late. If they comment on how busy you are, you've succeeded.

CALLING ALL FRIENDS

A good friend is there for you in time of need. Call one of them up and explain your situation, asking her to come over to your house before the parent drops her child off. Hopefully, when the parent sees your friend, she will realize that she is intruding and get the message that she's not welcome. If she doesn't get the message, have your friend step up and say, "It's nice meeting you. I'm so looking forward to some much-needed one-on-one time together while the kids play. I guess we'll see you in a few hours!"

DENIAL AIN'T JUST A RIVER IN EGYPT

Unfortunately, some parents—no matter how hard you try—are never going to get the message that you don't like them. In cases like this, there is no way around it; you're going to have to sit them down and have a face-to-face talk or at the very least a phone call. You don't have to get into specifics; you just need to make sure that they understand you're serious. Chances are, you're not the first parent to break up with them—and you won't be the last. In fact, don't be surprised if they move on to another parent immediately.

STEPS

1. **Give your kid's friend's parent the heads-up; you'd like to talk to her alone when she has time.**

2. **Set a time and place outside the hearing of your children.**

3. **Dump her without going into great detail. Be as honest as you feel comfortable being—depending on the situation. Keep it short and sweet, but to the point, placing as much blame on yourself.** *"There's no easy way to say this, but my schedule is so full right now that unfortunately I don't have time to hang out. I'm sorry if that sounds blunt or hurts*

your feelings. I just wanted to be clear with you, so that there won't be any misunderstandings and I won't disappoint you when I can't spend time at your house or mine to chat."

4. Allow her to respond, but try not to take care of her feelings. If she feels hurt, that's okay. Show compassion, but don't backpedal or allow her a way back into your life. One of her problems is not respecting your boundary, so if you allow her to break it now, it sends the message that you're not serious.

5. Apologize and make it clear that you don't want this to affect the children. You love her child and hope that Junior will continue to play with your child.

6. Get out. The longer you stay, the easier it is for the parent to suck you back in again.

7. Maintain your boundary. From this day forward, if you see the parent slipping, stay on top of it. Don't make exceptions, unless it's an emergency.

Tip: If the parent asks you whether she has done something wrong, think long and hard before telling her the truth. Ask yourself what purpose it will serve. Keep in mind that you still have to see her on a regular basis.

In a Pinch

COMPLAIN

As soon as your kid's friend's parent starts talking, complain. "You think your back hurts? Uch, mine is the worse. And it's not only my back; I've got these awful varicose veins in the back of my knee. Boy, are they a grisly, pulsating nightmare." Continue talking. Eventually she will find other things to do.

PUT HER TO WORK

Still can't ditch the parent? Next time she comes over and makes herself at home, tell her that it's cleaning day. If she doesn't leave right away, hand her a mop and bucket and put her to work. It shouldn't take long before she makes a break for it; if she still doesn't leave, at least you'll have a clean kitchen.

DUMPIPEDIA

▶ Parents' Day was established in 1994 and is held on the fourth Sunday of every July in the United States to recognize and support the role of parents in the rearing of children.

▶ The Parent-Teacher Association (or PTA) was founded in 1897 to bring together parents, teachers, and occasionally students within a particular school or school district, usually for fund-raising or discussion of issues related to the school.

▶ According to the U.S. Census Bureau, there are 82.5 million mothers in the United States and 66.3 million dads.

▶ The world's youngest parents were eight and nine years old, having their first child in China in 1910.

eight

THE LANDLORD

Signs It's Time to Dump Your Landlord

▶ You come home and find him fast asleep on your couch.

▶ Instead of fixing the broken elevator, he turns it into a storage closet.

▶ Your roach problem is so out of control, it's time to start collecting rent from the bugs.

▶ He's showing your apartment to potential tenants—and you didn't know you were moving out.

▶ He has you send your rent check directly to his bookie.

Putting the "Slum" in "Slumlord"

When I first got to Los Angeles, two of my sisters were already living there and were kind enough to let me live with them until I found an apartment. I wasn't entirely in love with Los Angeles and knew that unless I found the perfect apartment, I'd most likely be on the next plane back to New York. Having spent time in Los Angeles beforehand, I had my eye on one particular block—not just because people referred to it as the New York City street, but because it had the most beautiful chateau in the middle of a gorgeous, tree-lined road. I imagined that living there would be like living in France, and that the tenants drank wine each night as they discussed philosophers in the courtyard. When the day finally came that a "For Rent" sign appeared out front, I was all over it.

The apartment was a large one bedroom with two full bathrooms, each with the original 1930s tile and gorgeous art deco windows. This was it. This was the apartment I had to have. And then I met the landlord, Walter, who on a superficial level appeared normal despite his sailor shorts and lack of shirt. Little did I know that he was actually a certifiable kook. Ask him a question and he'd answer with something entirely different. When I inquired about the apartment, he answered by telling me that he was a Republican and an avid collector of guns. The only bit of information that I got out of him related to the apartment was that Richard Simmons apparently lived there in the 1970s, something that I got great joy from; so did all my friends, who surprised me with dolphin shorts for years to come.

Walter said a lot of things that day that should've roused my suspicions, but I chose to look the other way because I was so in love with the apartment. Little did I know that Walter was having a love affair of his own with the chateau. In fact, he was so possessive of the building that aside from allowing a gardener and cleaning crew to come in every few weeks, no one was allowed to touch his "baby." If there was a plumbing or electrical emergency, instead of having a professional come to fix it, Walter came himself. The problem was that Walter knew nothing about plumbing or electrical work; I suffered leaky faucets, a dripping shower, and no heat. When Walter discovered that my electric heaters were actually hooked up to the building's meter and not my personal meter, he entered my apartment without permission while I was at work and replaced them with tiny little electric heaters that looked like they'd be more at home in Barbie's Dream House than in my 1,000 sq. ft. apartment. They were nothing more than cheap props that feebly belched out cold air.

As the months passed, Walter's true colors were revealed, and he turned into a classic slumlord: handing out dirty buckets to those with leaks; issuing eviction notices to anyone who was more than three days late paying rent; and throwing away signs from the city notifying the tenants that Walter had stopped paying the chateau's electric bill and that the garage door opener and hallway lights were about to be shut off. My neighbors called the city's building inspectors and begged them to come out and investigate, but Walter must have been paying them off. Rumor had it that he even forged our signatures, saying that we had changed our minds and didn't want anyone from the housing authority to enter our apartments. The building was falling apart, fast.

Sensing that we were on to him, Walter became more paranoid by the minute. He decided that the only way to make sure no one from the housing authority snuck in was to always be at the building. This meant sleeping in the garage. To pass the time, he started collecting junk: old car engines, rotted canoes, and decayed stoves. He piled them all in the garage, making it increasingly difficult to park our vehicles.

And then the flood happened, destroying our cars and personal belongings stored in the garage. The junk that Walter had been collecting was piled so high over the drains that the storm water pouring into the garage had nowhere to go. Walter assured all of us during the storm that he was on top of the situation, placing sand bags and putting up a floodgate—but the truth was that he chose to go home to his family that night—and in order to avoid rush hour traffic, he stopped what he was doing and left.

It was official; my honeymoon with the chateau was over. I would not be drinking wine in the courtyard with my neighbors or talking about philosophers. My entire family and my friends begged me to move. Walter was not going to take responsibility, and he made that crystal clear. In addition, he made a point of telling me that if I tried to sue him, he would make living at the chateau unbearable for me. I told him I didn't appreciate threats, and he told me to keep my mouth shut if I wished to continue living there. I'd be lying if I said I wasn't scared.

A few months later, I had another surprise knock at my door. A realtor, along with twenty people wearing suits, wanted to look at my apartment. The realtor informed me that Walter wasn't the actual owner of the chateau—his mother was, and she had just died. As per the request of the rest of the family, the chateau was now for sale—despite Walter's protests.

The chateau was sold that day. Less than a week later, the new owner appeared along with a massive construction crew. He had big dreams for the chateau, including restoring it back to its original condition. As for Walter, he tried his best to hang on, unwilling to give up his love affair. He continued sleeping in a room off the garage until the new owner found out and changed the locks, notifying the police that Walter was not to come anywhere near the chateau. The possessive man who had let his baby fall apart, who had readily handed out eviction notices, had now been evicted from the building himself.

━━━━━

What I Learned

Slumlords get away with a lot because of weak tenants. I ought to know; I was one of them. I loved my apartment so much that I was willing to put up with no heat, a leaky shower, and a sink that constantly dripped. My friends would come over during the winter and start shivering. They asked me how on earth I put up with it. I tried my best to pretend it wasn't so bad—but it was. I knew Walter was in violation of countless laws, but I never took the time to look those laws up and know my rights. Why? Because he intimidated and threatened me. Had I known then what I know now, I wouldn't have hesitated in picking up that phone and getting someone from the city to come out and issue a citation, especially knowing how easy it is and how many resources are out there for mistreated tenants. I didn't know what a tenant association was, let alone how to organize one. Knowing what I know now, I would have started one in a heartbeat. It would have been a cinch, since everyone hated Walter. He was counting on us not doing anything, and assumed that if he stopped renting apartments to men (which he did) he would keep it that way. He knew it would be easier to bully women.

But I'm through with slumlords. While researching this chapter, I've become friendly with a few people in the housing department—all of whom have given me their business cards. My new landlord has started insinuating that he has plans to kick me out so he can jack up the rent. Little does he know that I have a handy little stack of business cards ready to call at the drop of a hat.

Laying the Groundwork

▸ If your landlord is harassing you, notify your local housing authorities immediately. The Fair Housing Act is a federal law that prohibits discrimination based on race, color, religion, sex, handicap, familial status, or national origin. Links to local housing authorities can be found on the Public Housing Authorities Directors Association Web site, www.PHADA.org.

▸ Never take what your landlord says as fact. Most landlords aren't up-to-date with housing laws and are counting on you not to question them.

▸ Familiarize yourself with your local housing laws. Most are available at your local library, or can be accessed online at www.FairHousingLaw.org.

▸ If your problems are serious—such as lack of heat, ineffective weather sealing, or locks that don't work—call the housing authority immediately and ask for the appropriate department to send someone out to inspect your home. For a list of nationwide housing authorities, go to www.affordablehousing online.com/housingauthoritysearch.asp.

▸ Study your lease. Most landlords use a standard lease form and add their own clauses to it; many are not legally binding.

▸ Start a file on your landlord. Document all issues and problems. Note the time and date of each incident, and save all the paperwork. Continue calling him. Landlords are notorious for telling authorities or a court that the tenant only complained once. This is when you pull out your files and start rattling off the dates of phone calls, letters written, and so forth. Oh, really? Just once? I don't think so.

▶ Write your landlord a certified letter with a return receipt. Include detailed information about the issues you're having and ask him to get back to you with a time and date when he will fix the problem. When possible, mention that if he doesn't fix the problem, it will get worse and become more costly to fix. Landlords don't want to spend any more money than they have to. Mention any dangers that could result in an injury. Keep in mind when writing the letter that this might become evidence if you go to court, so word the letter wisely.

▶ Pay your full rent on time. I know it's tempting to withhold rent or deduct expenses—referred to as the "repair and deduct" remedy—but housing lawyers generally advise against it. The reason is simple; landlords can sue tenants to recover the money or file an eviction action. If the tenant deducts money for repairs not covered by the remedy, the court may rule in favor of the landlord and require him to pay—or worse, allow the landlord to continue with the eviction process, since failure to pay rent is grounds for eviction. Unless you're absolutely certain that your expenses are covered by the remedy, pay your full rent. You can always get the money back by taking your landlord to court later.

Standard Legal Rights for Tenants

1. Limits on the amount of security deposit that a landlord can ask for.

2. Limits on the landlord's right to enter your unit.

3. Right to refund your security deposit.

4. Right to sue your landlord for violations of the law or your lease.

5. Right to withhold rent under certain circumstances.

6. Right to a habitable unit.

7. Protection against eviction.

Tip #1: Next time you move, make a point of talking to tenants in the building about your potential landlord. Ask how on top of maintenance he is. Your landlord may seem like the nicest person in the world, but the only way to know for sure is to discuss it with other tenants.

Tip #2: Get everything in writing with your landlord. Verbal agreements mean nothing. I once moved into an apartment that had a cabinet door that wouldn't open. My landlord promised to fix it before I moved in. I never got it in writing. During the entire four years that I lived there, he never fixed it.

How to Dump 'Em

MEET THE LANDLORD

After you've studied the laws in your city/state and familiarized yourself with the ones your landlord is in violation of, arrange for a meeting with him. Be clear about what you hope to accomplish in the meeting beforehand. Bring your folder of evidence to the meeting, including copies of certified letters written, the time and date of all phone calls to him, and photographs of any and all damage.

Warning: Yelling at your landlord will get you nowhere, and in most cases will only intensify his unwillingness to do anything.

1. Set up a meeting with your landlord.

2. Tell him why you're there and what you hope to accomplish. *"I'm here to talk about my bathroom sink, which has been dripping for months. My goal is to get the issue resolved in a timely fashion."*

3. Present your file. *"Here's my folder with photographs showing the damage, as well as certified letters that I have sent informing you of the situation."*

4. Let your landlord respond. Listen to everything he has to say before speaking. If he responds with excuses, gently remind him of the laws he is breaking. Remember, he's counting on your ignorance.

5. If your landlord agrees to handle the problem, get a time and date and ask for it in writing. If he won't agree to put it in writing, let him know that you're adding it to your file.

6. If he doesn't agree to fix the problem, tell him that you'll be handing your file over to the housing authorities.

Tip: If the problem(s) you're having with your landlord affect other tenants, consider organizing a tenant association. For information about starting a tenant association, check out www.tenant.net. Applying pressure to your landlord as an entire building carries more weight with the city. Set up a meeting with all the affected tenants, take notes of the issues discussed, and then send a copy to your landlord. Let him know you mean business.

BREAK THE LEASE

Dump your landlord by breaking your lease early. Most likely you will incur a penalty, such as losing your security deposit or having to pay out the remaining months of your lease. However, if you're living in uninhabitable conditions, you might be legally allowed to terminate your lease without having to pay a dime. Visit www.fairhousinglaw.org for your local and state fair housing enforcement agencies and laws. This site also provides the names and numbers of legal aids and bar associations that help low-income families for little to no fee. Another Web site to check out is the Department of Housing and Urban Development's, also known as HUD (www.hud.gov). It enforces the federal fair housing laws, which prohibit discrimination. In situations where you're living in an apartment with mold, without heat or running water, or in a building that is unsafe (such as a unit with a broken lock or broken hallway light), your landlord might very well be in violation of the law, meaning that your lease is no longer legal and binding.

MEDIATOR

Before taking your landlord to court, ask whether he would be willing to sit down with a mediator, a neutral third person chosen by both tenant and landlord. Mediators meet with both parties and formulate a voluntary solution to a dispute; many are publicly funded and are available for free or at a low cost. To find one in your area, call your mayor's or city manager's office and ask for a mediator to help resolve a landlord dispute. They can also be found in the Yellow Pages under "mediation services."

C U IN COURT

Going to court should be your last resort; however, if your rights have been violated repeatedly and your landlord continues not to do anything, it should be an option. The good news is that many courts provide free services that help you through the process, including filing your proper paperwork. You can also contact law libraries and ask for referrals for free or low-cost legal assistance services. If you decide to go to court, bring as much evidence as possible, including the originals of all documents. Take a witness with you if you can. If your witness can't attend, have him write a letter. Most landlord disputes can be handled in small claims court, including getting back your security deposit. The maximum amount you can sue for differs from state to state, but usually ranges from $3,000 to $10,000, and it's relatively inexpensive to file a claim. Call your local court and ask what the procedure is. Check out www.nolo.com for a wealth of information on landlords, lawyers, and the legal process.

In a Pinch

STRIPES

Join the military and say good-bye to your lease. Tell your landlord that you just got official orders transferring you out of the country—then mention the Soldiers' and Sailors' Civil Relief Act, which allows you to break a lease. Salute and leave.

TEXT MESSAGE BREAKUP

Text message your landlord and give him the news. Try, "U2LYK IN 30 DAYZ IM OUT. L8R."

Q. *Why are some people afraid of their landlords?*
A. Landlords have a lot of power over their tenants. Most people use their apartments as their place of rest, where they can escape from their troubles. But when their homes are threatened by eviction, poor maintenance, an intrusive landlord, or something else, tenants are unable to rest and relax. They fear for the security of one of life's basic needs: shelter!

Q. *What's one of the biggest mistakes people make with their landlords?*
A. There are two big mistakes tenants commonly make. One is not paying the rent; the other is not paying the full rent on time, especially when it becomes a habit. This can result in late fees, and sometimes the landlord will evict a tenant because a late-paying tenant is a pain.

Q. *What are the most common problems with landlords?*
A. Poor maintenance. This is especially true for "mom-and-pop" landlords who only own one or two properties. They often aren't trained property managers, and sometimes they don't want to incur expenses or go to the trouble of fixing small problems. Other common problems are landlords who get mad at their tenants and take out their frustrations on them.

Q. *What's the best way to approach a landlord about a problem?*

A. Usually the best approach is something written, dated, and signed, describing the problem, how it affects you, and asking for a specific solution. Keep a copy of the note so you'll have some proof of when and what you told the landlord. Be direct and polite, and don't threaten or accuse. If the problem is a continuing one, you can point out that fact very simply: "As I indicated in my note of January 4, the roof is leaking. Water has dripped onto some of my clothes and damaged them. Please fix the roof as soon as possible. Here is a receipt for $35 for dry cleaning clothes that were leaked on; please reimburse me as soon as possible. I have stopped using the closet where the leak is, in order to avoid further damage, but I would like to be able to use that closet again soon. Thank you."

A lot of people want to intimidate their landlords and try to do so by copying their complaint letters to an attorney and writing "cc: Mr. Attorney, Esq." on the bottom of the letter. Some people like to explain in their letter that they've spoken to an attorney or that they know their rights or something like that. I see no point in doing that. If you have a reasonable landlord, the fact that the landlord knows you have an attorney will make no difference in the way she reacts to your letter. If your landlord is unreasonable, she'll just get angry. In either case, you'll be marked as potential trouble, and the landlord will start marshalling her defenses and calling her lawyer.

Q. *Is there a law that says how many days a landlord has to take care of an issue?*

A. Laws can vary from state to state and even from city to city, but in most states the answer is yes. Often, the landlord is given a "reasonable" amount of time to address a problem, and what's reasonable may depend on the problem. Garbage overflowing from a garbage can onto the walkway can usually be fixed pretty quickly, but a roof leak in the middle of winter when there aren't any roofing contractors available may take longer.

Q. *What can someone do after that time has passed and there's been no change?*
A. That depends on the applicable law. Usually the tenant can deduct a reasonable amount from the rent payment to compensate for the decrease in housing services. For instance, if the heater doesn't work, the tenant might be justified in withholding 30 percent of the rent, especially when the weather is cold. It's best to check local laws before withholding any rent—there may be limits on the types of things for which a tenant can withhold rent, or there may be a requirement that the tenant give notice in some fashion before withholding rent. If you are going to withhold rent, be sure to send the landlord a note with the partial rent payment saying how much you are withholding and why—if you have tried to get the landlord to fix the problem before but the landlord was unresponsive, briefly and politely recite that history in the note.

Q. *How do you dump your landlord?*
A. If your lease is expired or you are on a month-to-month, week-to-week, or day-to-day tenancy, it's pretty easy; give notice and then leave. If you are in the middle of a lease, it can be a bit trickier. You are legally responsible for paying the rent during the entire term of the lease. This sounds bleak, but there's a little hope. Even if you break the lease, the landlord has an obligation to try to mitigate their damages—that is, they have to act reasonably to re-rent the apartment.

Always give the landlord plenty of notice before you move out, even if you are breaking the lease. That way the landlord can market the apartment sooner and maybe even have someone ready to move in when you move out, eliminating lost rent damages. If you can find a qualified replacement tenant and introduce that person to the landlord when you give notice, that would also be great.

Q. *What's the best way for a tenant to stay informed and know his rights?*
A. I would start with local tenants' rights organizations. There are a number of them, particularly in major cities, and they almost all maintain up-to-date Web sites. Lots of tenants' rights organizations hold lectures and workshops, usually for free (the lecturers are often tenants' rights attorneys fishing for new clients, but they'll be glad to help you even if you are not a potential client). Most cities that have rent control will make their rent control ordinance available on the Internet and will also have a rent board, which may have its own Web site.

Q. *What's the best way of making sure you get your security deposit back?*
A. Give sufficient notice before you vacate, even if you are vacating at the end of your lease. Thirty days' notice is usually sufficient, but a little more is usually better. Do it in writing, and keep a copy. Try to schedule an end-of-lease walkthrough with your landlord so you can both look at the place after you've got your stuff out of it. You can document the move-out condition with photographs or a video. If the landlord tries to keep some or all of your deposit, get an itemized list of why (the landlord is usually required by law to provide this within several weeks of the time you vacate the apartment). Look over the list. Are the claims legitimate and reasonable? If so, be prepared for those to be deducted. If you disagree with the landlord's deductions, write a letter. Remember, it's addressed for the landlord but it's written for the court—because if you get no satisfaction from the landlord here, the next step is to go to court. And finally, if you want the landlord to return the security deposit,

you have to tell the landlord where to send it. This may seem elementary, but it's pretty common that people forget to do this. If you don't want the landlord to know where you will be living, have her send the deposit refund to a friend.

Q. *When should a tenant take his landlord to court?*
A. If the landlord is not taking you or the problem seriously and if you don't see a good faith effort by the landlord to resolve the problem, then you have the option to sue. If you wait, you may forget some crucial fact, you may lose some evidence, or your witnesses may forget something. Also, if you wait, the court may wonder why you waited—maybe the problem isn't really so big after all. When the problem arises after the tenancy has ended— like your landlord is wrongfully withholding part of your security deposit or you had to move out because the place was in terrible condition and you want a partial rent refund—then there is really no reason to delay at all. If the problem is a small one and you continue to live in the unit, then you may want to delay a little in order to protect your relationship with your landlord. But think about what delay tells the landlord—you won't act to protect yourself. This could make the landlord's behavior get even worse. And do you really want to continue to live in a place where the landlord doesn't take your complaints seriously?

Q. *Who was the better landlord, Mr. Roper or Mr. Furley?*
A. I have to go with Mr. Furley on this one. Mr. Roper was just not good when it came to dealing with issues. Mr. Furley, on the other hand, was responsive—not to mention colorful. He never gave up.

DUMPIPEDIA

▶ New York City's most famous landlord, Donald Trump, dumped TV sidekick Carolyn Kepcher from his show *The Apprentice* in 2006.

▶ Norman Fell won a Golden Globe for playing landlord Mr. Roper on *Three's Company*.

▶ Land-lording is said to have started during the Roman Empire, when peasants were bound to the land and dependent on their landlords for protection.

▶ The Fair Housing Act was signed on April 11, 1968, by which U.S. president?
  A. Richard Nixon
  B. Lyndon Johnson
  C. John F. Kennedy

The correct answer is B. Lyndon Johnson.

nine

THE FRIEND

Signs It's Time to Dump Your Friend

▶ She goes to the bathroom every time the check arrives.

▶ She gives you hand-me-downs, but never without saying, "Here, take this. It's huuuuuge on me."

▶ She calls you her best friend, but she doesn't even know your last name.

▶ Her favorite movie is *Single White Female*, and she starts looking more and more like you every day.

▶ You're one of the ten lucky people she forwards chain letters to.

Best Friends for Never

My first best friend was named Sydney. I found out we were best friends when she announced it to our third grade class. I had just moved to New Hampshire and was in the market for new friends. Sydney staked her claim during third period's Show and Tell. She stood up, took my hand, held it high in the air—the way a boxing referee holds a fighter's hand when he declares victory—and presented me as her "show." Then she proceeded to "tell" my class that I was now spoken for. The day ended at her house, where she stabbed both of our index fingers with her mother's sewing needle, forcefully pressed them together, and pronounced us "blood sisters." The next day at school, Sydney gleefully showed off her index finger (now wrapped in a Smurf Band-Aid) to all the adoring kids on the playground.

Little did she know that there would be some stiff competition for my friendship. I was fresh meat, and kids were lining up at recess to be my friends. I was so popular, in fact, that invitations poured in for sleepovers and birthday parties. The same could not be said for poor Sydney, who was so pissed off about my busy social calendar that she decided to show her anger by pulling out a chunk of my hair.

Things continued to get worse when she made a point of scaring away the other kids who approached me in the schoolyard, something that did not sit well with me. I was afraid of asking her to back off for fear she would kick me in the shins, so I kept my mouth shut. The other kids told me the only way to make it official that she was no longer my best friend—or any kind of friend, for that matter—was to have a schoolyard fight, but I was having none of that. It wasn't my style—not to mention that she was at least twice my size.

Instead, I stopped talking to her and didn't invite her to my very first sleepover party. Unfortunately, that didn't stop her from showing up anyway along with her down-filled Holly Hobbie sleeping bag. My other friends asked her to leave, but she refused. Clearly I was too scared to ask her myself. Finally, after a long staring contest, she gave her ultimatum. She'd leave, but only after I thumb wrestled her. I didn't get the point of thumb wrestling, but if that's what it would take, then thumbs away!

The count began. "One, two, three four, I declare a thumb war!" And in one fell swoop, Sydney snapped my right thumb backward, spraining it instantly and forcing me to walk around for weeks with a giant bubble cast. And with that, she was out of my life forever.

What I Learned

I should have told Sydney that I didn't appreciate her pulling out chunks of my hair and that because of it, I wasn't going to invite her to my slumber party. Most likely she didn't know that kicking and pulling someone's hair out is no way to keep a friend.

I've dumped my share of casual friends over the years. Some I avoided, others I lashed out at hoping they'd dump me. I even moved cross-country without telling some of them. But the most painful and difficult breakups I've had to go through are the ones between me and my best friends. When I've been the one deciding to dump my friend, I usually did it one of two ways: either I'd lash out over something that had nothing to do with what I was really upset about, or I'd become less available to my friend and make up some kind of white lie, thinking I was sparing her feelings. Speaking to people for this chapter and reflecting back on all the friends I have dumped, I now realize that despite having the best of intentions, I most likely hurt my former friends a lot. No one deserves to walk around not knowing what she did wrong in a relationship. Sydney, if you're reading this, I'm sorry.

Laying the Groundwork

▶ Write a list of the things you don't like about your friend. Then walk away from the list for a day or two.

▶ When you're ready, look at the list and revise it. Are you irritated by the sound of her voice, or does her tone come across as condescending, making you feel constantly judged? You don't want to lose a good friend because of a superficial annoyance.

▶ Consider taking a temporary break. Absence makes the heart grow fonder. Allow yourself some time to reflect before making any final decisions.

▶ Warn her. Give her a heads-up, and explain what's bothering you. Be clear about what your issues are and what you'd like to change.

▶ Allow her to express her issues with you.

▶ Think about other friends who might be affected by your breakup. Are you willing to say good-bye to those friends? Be careful not to put them in the middle.

▶ Rehearse what you're going to say. Do not speak for anyone other than yourself. It may be tempting to say, "I'm not the only person who feels this way," but that's not your place. If your other friend has an issue, let her speak for herself.

▶ Come up with a potential meeting place. Try a park, café, or restaurant where neither of you has a history. The last thing you want is to meet her at your favorite breakfast joint and then be reminded of her every time you eat there.

▶ Make it your goal to end things on a good note and not burn bridges.

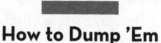

How to Dump 'Em

THE TIES THAT NO LONGER BIND

Friendships come in many shapes and forms. While the casual ones don't always require a lot of work, the more personal ones often do. When breaking up with a close friend, gather your courage and tell her, so she doesn't feel abandoned by you. However, if your friend has betrayed you, all bets are off.

Caution: Be gentle. It hurts to be broken up with; treat your friend the way you would want to be treated. This is not about blaming her, it's about saying good-bye, so be as honest as you can, speak your truth, and pepper it with kindness.

STEPS

1. **Call and arrange for a meeting or phone call. Let your friend know that you'd like to talk to her about your friendship. If she asks whether anything's wrong, tell her you want to talk openly and honestly about your relationship. Avoid getting into a serious discussion in that moment, as people often react with panic.**

2. **Thank her for meeting or talking with you.**

3. **Start with a compliment or something positive. Try, *"You're one of the funniest people I know."***

4. **Dump her.** *"There's no easy way to say this, but after carefully thinking about our relationship, I've decided to end it. I'm sorry. There are many things I will miss."*

5. **Let her respond.** You owe it to her to listen to how she feels, but that doesn't have to change the way you feel. Be strong. She will want an explanation; give your most important reasons. Don't try to teach her any lessons. This is not the time to judge or blame her.

6. **Take responsibility for any hurt you've caused.**

7. **Put closure on the conversation. Make it clear what you wish to have happen. Never see her again? Don't be vague, as it will only give her reason to hope that you'll change your mind.**

8. **Wish her well.**

DOWNGRADE

Not all friendships have to be black and white. Try dumping your friend by downgrading her from a close friend to more of an acquaintance. This option works well for those wishing to break up with someone who's part of a larger circle of friends. A big advantage of the downgrade is that there's always room for an upgrade, so that if in the future you want to bump her up again, you can.

The way to shift the dynamic is by not avoiding her when she calls—just be less available to get together. Try and see her with your mutual friends. The hope is to cut back on your time spent together without your friend noticing. Be prepared, however, to answer her questions if she calls you on it. Explain that all friendships go through transitions and for you this is one of those times. If she still wants answers, let her down gently. For example, "I'm looking for a way that we can remain in each other's life, but in a less time-consuming way, since my plate is beyond full right now."

DEAR JOHN

Breaking up with a friend who is a better communicator than you are or who has a super strong personality is extra difficult, especially if you fear that you will shut down emotionally. In these cases, it's okay to write her a letter or e-mail. Word your note carefully, and allow your friend to respond if she needs to. Keep in mind that having a conversation with your friend in person allows you the opportunity to potentially gain insight that might lead you to decide that you don't want to dump her after all. A letter or e-mail is more final. If that's what you want, give your friend as much closure as possible. When applicable, wish her happiness and let her know that when you look back on your friendship, you'll focus on the good times.

SLOW FADE AWAY

A popular choice for many, including myself at one time, the slow fade away should only be used with casual friends—closer friends don't tend to go away that easily, at least not without some kind of explanation. The slow fade away involves distancing yourself by not returning your friend's calls, ignoring her text messages and e-mails, cancelling plans the two of you have made, and hoping that she eventually gets the hint and goes away. The main problem with this breakup is that unless you both want to dump each other, only one of you knows that the relationship is over. This means your friend will most likely keep calling you until she has an explanation. Be prepared to make it more official if your friend calls you on it.

In a Pinch

SIGN UP AS GUESTS ON THE *JERRY SPRINGER SHOW*

Nothing quite says, "We're through" like a live studio audience. Dump your friend on the *Jerry Springer Show*. Check out www .JerrySpringerTV.com and see what shows producers are currently casting for. If you don't see an episode about friends, suggest one. They are anxiously standing by, looking for their next great episode.

COUPLES' THERAPY, ANYONE?

Therapy has helped save many relationships; why not let it save yours? Tell your friend that you're unhappy with your relationship and suggest that the two of you work it out in therapy. Throw in that you're willing to go twice a week just to get things started, but would be open to taking it to three to four sessions a week. Suggest going to coffee after your sessions in order to process the issues brought up during your appointments.

CONSTANT CALLER

If you still can't shake your friend, take it up a notch by forcing her to dump you. Call her constantly, just to talk. Try monopolizing the conversation, and when she tries to get a word in edgewise, talk over her. Call her up in the middle of the night and tell her that you couldn't sleep because you couldn't remember her favorite number. Two thousand and three, right? The next night, call again, this time telling her that you have no idea what her favorite dim sum dish is. Pork buns? Give it a week and she'll be done with you.

DUMPIPEDIA

▸ In 2005, BFFs Nicole Richie and Paris Hilton dumped each other.

▸ National Friendship Day is the first Sunday in August and was officially declared a holiday in the United States by Congress in 1935.

▸ In 1997, the United Nations named Winnie the Pooh the world's Ambassador of Friendship.

▸ Research shows that good friends help you live longer. In fact, Australian scientists have shown that friends do more for your life expectancy than family.

▸ According to research by the University of Oregon, one-third of all preschool kids have an imaginary friend.

▸ What year did "That's What Friends Are For" win the Grammy for Song of the Year?
  A. 1985
  B. 1986
  C. 1987

The answer is B. 1986.

part three
TAKING CARE OF BUSINESS

ten

THE ASSISTANT

Signs It's Time to Dump Your Assistant

▸ You ask her to do something and she says, "No thanks, I'm good."

▸ You hear her snoring from the next room.

▸ She asks *you* for an assistant.

▸ She goes to get coffee . . . and returns two hours later without the coffee and carrying shopping bags from Urban Outfitters.

▸ She calls in sick to work and you turn on the TV and see her dancing in the audience of the *Ellen* show.

That Will Be All

I've only had one personal assistant. His name was French Fry, and I'd tell you his real name, only I never actually found out, since he had it legally changed. At the time I was producing music videos in Manhattan. I had just left the world of documentary filmmaking, a job that—although stressful in its own way—was nothing compared to the insanity of the music video world, where artists demand anything and everything and refuse to take no for an answer.

On one such job, I sat listening to a hugely successful rapper as he discussed his vision for his new music video. It was his directorial debut, and he wanted to go big: really big. I'm talking helicopters, pimped-out cars, dancers, and pyrotechnics. I sat furiously scribbling my notes, making sure to give the stink eye to the executive producer every chance I got. One of those glances I mouthed, "I can't do this."

To which he leaned in and whispered, "Don't worry, I'll get you an assistant."

The next second, from across the room I heard, "I'll do it!" All eyes turned to French Fry, all 6 feet 3 inches, 280 pounds of him. He had a hard look to him, with scars on his face that I'm pretty sure didn't get there from acne. He was a member of the rapper's posse.

"Done," said the rapper. "French Fry it is, now it's hot as hell in here and I want to go home. What's next?"

"Wait!" I shouted followed by a dimpled smile. "Hold on a sec. If you don't mind, I'd feel more comfortable interviewing a few other people before—"

But I didn't get the chance to finish my sentence—the executive producer cut me off with, "We're all set. Continue. French Fry's great." Excuse me? What just happened here?! I glanced over at French Fry, who was either smiling at me or sucking food out of his teeth. It could have gone either way. The deal was done; French Fry would start the following day and pick me up at home at 7:30 a.m.

The next morning I woke up fully expecting to jump in a cab to get to work. I wasn't holding my breath that anyone named after a fried potato was going to actually show up. But at 7:29 a.m. he was at my door, holding a latte and a cranberry scone. Unfortunately, they were both for him, but it was okay—he was on time, and that's all that really mattered.

Our drive to work caught me completely off guard. Looking at him you'd swear he wasn't a talker, but during that drive to work he did nothing but talk. He gave me a glimpse into the life of French Fry. He grew up in the Bronx, lived next door to the rapper whose video we were making, was raised by a single mother and older sister, and as a boy he cried—a lot. His sister, looking for a way to stop his crying, stuck a french fry in his mouth— and the rest was history. I learned a lot about French Fry in those twenty minutes; I learned that although he presented himself to the world as a toughie, he was actually a softie with a heart of gold. I liked him. I seriously liked him.

From the moment we arrived at the office, French Fry hit the ground running. Helicopters, dancers, locations: you name it, he got it done. He was my man, never once complaining about the outrageous hours we were putting in. Twenty-hour days were standard those first few weeks. But we were doing it, totally in sync. We were an unlikely pair, the two of us, but we made it work beautifully. It wasn't long before our co-workers got sick of our annoying habit of finishing each other's sentences. "Remember that time that we"—and French Fry would raise his hand and drop it—his version of a laugh. When an obstacle appeared, French Fry would nod his head and say, "Got it covered." Then he covered it. It was that easy.

I would not have survived those summer months without French Fry. He was my rock—my knight in shining armor. But as the summer came to a close, the music video jobs stopped coming in. By the time the leaves had started to fall off the trees, there wasn't a lot to do around the office.

Then on a cold and bitter day, while French Fry was out on an errand, my boss sat me down for a talk. I knew instantly by the look on his face what was coming next. French Fry had to be let go. My heart sank. My boss thought that since we were so close, I should be the one to do it. He was right, but the twenty-four-year-old in me just couldn't bear it. "Me?! I don't think so. No!" I said. My head was spinning. How do you fire the best assistant ever? Screw assistant, French Fry was my friend. There were times I felt I was assisting him. I knew his mother and sister. We'd been in the trenches together. I was sick to my stomach. There was no way I could do it, so I begged my boss to do it until he agreed. I knew I was wrong.

The next morning, as I sat at my desk staring at my latte and raspberry scone (courtesy of French Fry), the door to our tiny conference room was closed—the same room in which I first laid eyes on him. When it opened, French Fry appeared. He walked slowly toward my desk, looked straight into my eyes, heart-broken. He took one deep breath, exhaled, and said, "I thought we were friends?" I jumped up from my desk, desperately wanting to hug him, but held myself back.

"We are!" I pleaded.

But he shook his head in dismay and replied, "No. We're not." And with that French Fry walked out the door and out of my life—forever.

What I Learned

After French Fry, I worked on a few more commercials and music videos before hanging up my producing hat. On those jobs, I had to exercise my firing muscle. The way I did it was by making sure everyone knew what their job was and what was expected of them on day one. I was their leader, plain and simple. If they slacked, I'd warn them, and if they failed to correct the problem, I'd fire them. Yes, I, the avoidant girl, fired people.

Not having the courage to fire French Fry ate at me for months. There were so many times I just wanted to pick up the phone and call him. But I never did. I lost a friend, and I finally understood that the problem was that we *were* friends. French Fry and I were off and running without any kind of conversation about what my expectations and boundaries were. I couldn't fire him because I never really felt like his boss—that was my fault, not his. When I interviewed assistants and bosses for this chapter—some happy, some not so happy—I learned that the best relationships are the ones in which the roles have been clearly defined. A few bosses I spoke to even have check-ins with their assistants, making sure everyone is on the same page. It gives them an opportunity to clear the air and move on instead of holding on to resentment. I'll never make the mistake I made with French Fry again. I miss you, French Fry, and if you're reading this, I'm sorry I let you down.

Laying the Groundwork

▶ Start keeping a list of problems you have with your assistant. Look for patterns over time.

▶ Study any contracts signed between you and your assistant. Wrongful termination lawsuits are becoming commonplace, so consult a lawyer if needed.

▶ If you have a human resources department, notify it as early as possible, as there are specific rules in place to handle these situations and HR usually needs to build a paper case in order to justify the firing.

▶ Give your assistant at least one warning, citing examples of things she's doing wrong. Make it clear that things need to change if she wants to keep her job.

▶ Decide what kind of severance pay you wish to give as well as any other continued benefits, if applicable.

▶ Back up all her computer files. Disgruntled assistants have been known to delete files out of spite.

▶ Be ready to change her computer password.

▶ Take inventory of all company items still in her possession including credit cards, cell phones, computers, company cars, and office keys. Decide on the best time to recover them.

▶ Choose a day you want your assistant to leave: two weeks later, or by the end of the day?

▶ Come up with a time and place to dump her. Experts suggest the end of the day, in a neutral setting such as a conference room. This allows your assistant to be alone in order to collect herself.

▶ Make it your goal to have your assistant leave with her ego intact.

How to Dump 'Em

READY, AIM, FIRE!

By now you've already given your assistant at least one warning, so she shouldn't be totally surprised when you ask to talk to her. Remember, this is business, so be professional. Getting emotional or making excuses can be perceived as weak and unprofessional. Keep in mind that other people are going to hear how you handled your assistant's termination, so make sure you do it properly. Speak clearly and straightforwardly, and show empathy.

STEPS

1. **Pick a time and a place to sit your assistant down.**

2. **Start with a compliment or something positive. Try,** *"Your upbeat and positive attitude has certainly been an asset to our office."* **Do not start by asking her a question such as** *"How are things at home?"*

3. **Identify the times you've warned her. Try,** *"However, as you know, there have been a number of times when I've brought to your attention my need for ____."*

4. **Bring up the importance of the issue. Try,** *"As you know, the field I'm in requires an enormous amount of ____."*

5. **Fire her.** *"Unfortunately, because I have not been getting that from you, I'm afraid I'm going to have to let you go."* **If you can, offer to write her a letter of recommendation.**

6. **Allow your assistant to have her reaction, but don't get sucked into it emotionally. She might not be able to understand or agree with your decision, but she doesn't have**

to. *"It's just not working out, I'm sorry,"* is okay. This is business. Show compassion, but don't feel so bad that you give her the job back. You must be firm in your decision.

HAVE HUMAN RESOURCES OR A FIRING SPECIALIST DO IT FOR YOU

If you have an HR department, chances are the staff is trained in handling employee termination and will do it with or for you. If you don't have an HR team, one way to avoid a wrongful termination lawsuit is to turn to a consulting firm that specializes in firing employees. Consultants help limit your legal liability as well as structure severance pay packages. They'll train you to fire your assistant, as well as actually do it for you.

HIRE A VIRTUAL ASSISTANT

Virtual assistants (VAs) are gaining popularity. They are trained professionals who work from another location, either at home or in an office, some in cities miles away from where you reside. VAs communicate through e-mail, phone, fax, snail mail, or diskette, in addition to using Web-based tools such as instant messaging. Most handle basic word processing, phone answering, bill paying, appointment scheduling, and calendar maintenance, but you can train them to go beyond administrative duties to client development and marketing support. For more information, check out the International Virtual Assistants Association at www.ivaa.org. The site will help you locate a VA who's right for you. Then dump your current assistant by telling her that due to financial cutbacks, a virtual assistant has been hired to take over her position.

In a Pinch

THE SECRET

Buy your assistant a copy of the book *The Secret* and tell her to visualize a new job because she no longer has one in your office.

DUMPIPEDIA

▶ The *Wall Street Journal* reported that legendary film producer Scott Rudin has dumped over 250 personal assistants.

▶ The *New York Times* reported that in 2006, Radio Shack fired four hundred employees in its Fort Worth headquarters by means of an e-mail that read, "The workforce reduction notification is currently in progress. Unfortunately, your position is one that has been eliminated."

▶ Administrative Professionals Day, formerly known as National Secretary's Day, was created in 1952 by Harry F. Klemfuss of the advertising firm Young and Rubicam. It is observed on the Wednesday of the last full week of April, and recognizes the work of secretaries, administrative assistants, and receptionists.

eleven

THE CO-WORKER

Signs It's Time to Dump Your Co-worker

▶ He clicks his pen to the tune of "The Star-Spangled Banner."

▶ He sucks food out of his teeth all day long, also to the tune of "The Star-Spangled Banner."

▶ He clips his nails and flings the clippings over the cubicle wall, onto your "To Do" pile.

▶ He calls everyone at the office either Joanie or Chachi.

▶ You go into the office kitchen and find him drinking milk from the carton.

Mind Your Own Ps and Cubicles

The summer before entering college, I worked for a telephone answering service in New Hampshire. This entailed sitting in a cubicle in front of a computer screen and waiting patiently for people to call local businesses whose phones were re-routed to our screens. The unwritten rules were relatively simple; chitchat was for the break room, and talking on the floor should be kept to a minimum.

Things were rolling along great until Konnie "with a K" showed up. Yes, Konnie with a K. Konnie with a K was the most aggressively incompetent woman I'd ever met. She spoke with a thick New Hampshire accent that only a mother could love, and, as luck would have it, Konnie with a K lived with her mother. For those not familiar with the New Hampshire accent, try dropping the letter "R" completely from your vocabulary and you'll have a pretty good idea. For example, I thought Konnie's last name was Mah until I saw it written down and realized that it was actually Moore.

Rumor around the office was that Konnie's mouth anatomically would not close. Even while waiting for the phone to ring, she sat with her mouth open as if waiting to catch a grape tossed by a co-worker across the room. Konnie had zero interest in the rules of the office, blabbing away to and at everyone, regardless of whether they were listening. She'd talk about her mother, "Oh, my mah is wicked ahsum. She's such a troopah, havin ahthritus and all. I mean, ain't nuthin' stops huh."

Konnie also loved to talk about her boyfriend, Stevie, and what a great "lovah" he was. But her favorite "little lovah" was her kitty cat, Angela Lansbury; it turned out that Konnie had a thing for *Murder, She Wrote*. She loved her cat so much that she even had a small tattoo of Angela Lansbury on her ankle, something she was only too proud to show us at least twice a day.

When the phone wasn't ringing at the office (and she wasn't exhausting us with her mindless gab), Konnie talked baby talk with Stevie and Angela Lansbury. I tried pointing out that personal phone calls were strictly forbidden, but she'd shoo me away with her hand, having no interest in me or anyone else in the office. She also had the strangest sneeze I'd ever heard. When she sneezed, she said "Q." Yes, the letter Q. Konnie with a K sneezed Qs, and never just one—they always came in fives.

The days were longer and more frustrating with Konnie working beside us. We left her a few notes asking her politely to take her personal calls in the break room, as the constant distraction was making it hard for us to get our jobs done, but Konnie used the notes to put her used gum in before throwing them in the trash.

One day, Konnie's voice was so loud it prevented the rest of us from picking up our phones. When she shouted, "Now can you hear me?" for the third time, I stood up and leaned into her cubicle. It turned out Konnie had the mouth piece on her headset pointed on top of her head, instead of directly in front of her mouth. I explained the proper position, but Konnie couldn't care less, aggressively explaining that her way was actually the proper way.

It seemed the more we tried clueing Konnie in to her disruptive behavior, the angrier she got. Finally one of the women I worked with spoke to the supervisor about Konnie, but he just looked at us blankly and said, "Girl stuff. Work it out."

The next day, I set a plan in motion that I'm not too proud of—but summer was winding down and I was leaving for college anyway. Each night, at 11 p.m. sharp, a pervert caller would ring one of the doctor's offices (whose phone we answered) and ask the girls what we were wearing. We were under strict orders to hang up the phone immediately or be fired. Management knew whether we complied, as all calls were recorded. At 10:56 p.m. the next night, Konnie was lured into the kitchen with an invitation to enjoy a piece of homemade key lime pie. Never one to turn down free food, especially pie, Konnie leapt from her seat. This was my cue to jump into Konnie's cubicle, where I planted myself in her chair and waited for the phone to ring. At 11:00 p.m., the phone rang. I picked up Konnie's phone and answered in my thickest New Hampshire accent, and instead of hanging up, I listened. I listened to him talk about what he was wearing; where he was; what he was going to do next. And I kept on listening, throwing in an occasional "ewww!" and "ahhh!" Three minutes later, the ordeal was over. Konnie with a K was fired two days later.

Much like a cat, Konnie landed on her feet. I heard that soon after she was fired, she and her mother were selling bejeweled "Kat Kollars," with a K, at a kiosk in the Mall of New Hampshire.

What I Learned

I should have made more of an effort with Konnie and discussed more productive ways for us to work together, not taken the easy way out and gotten her fired. I'd like to say it was because I was eighteen years old, but the truth is, I might have done that six months ago. I'm not good at hiding my feelings when I don't like someone. Case in point, I'm an eye roller—so unless you're blind, you're going to know if I don't like you. I work hard at not being so black and white in my thinking, but it's difficult. I've had plenty of annoying co-workers in my life, and in too many of those cases, I let my resentment build and build until I exploded. Not so healthy, and at times embarrassing.

Researching this chapter has shown me that it doesn't pay to resent your co-worker. The only way to get your co-worker to stop doing something is to talk to him, not roll your eyes or sigh. Show compassion and have the patience to gently remind him when he's behaving inappropriately, not verbally assault him. "Nudging" is what my Nana liked to call it.

Laying the Groundwork

▶ Before dumping your co-worker, check around and make sure that you aren't the only one who has a problem with him. If you notice the rest of the office giving him high fives and laughing at his jokes, you might want to ask yourself whether perhaps *you* are the annoying co-worker.

▶ Document things carefully, providing as much information as possible. This is especially helpful for those of you with co-workers who are loved by the higher-ups and have a way of blaming you for all their mistakes. By keeping memos on your co-workers and their mistakes, you build evidence that you can present if push comes to shove and you find yourself sitting in your boss's office having to defend yourself.

▶ Write a list of things your co-worker does that bother you.

▶ Now come up with a pared-down version. You have to pick your battles, so stick to the big issues and let the others take a back seat.

▶ Ask yourself whether there's anything you're doing to encourage his behavior—and stop doing it. For instance, if you're annoyed by a chatty co-worker, have you been providing an ear for him?

- Rehearse what you're going to say. Play out different scenarios and try and guess what your co-worker's reaction might be and how best to handle it.

- Be prepared for your co-worker to pull out his own list of issues.

- Don't involve the rest of the office. This is between you and your co-worker—and no one else.

- Scope out a neutral location, away from your other co-workers, to talk to him.

How to Dump 'Em

Caution: Tread carefully, because most likely your co-worker has no idea what's about to come.

WE NEED TO TALK

One of the most common mistakes people make when sitting down with their co-workers is apologizing for their words. Telling your annoying co-worker not to take what you're saying personally only weakens your message. Keep the conversation as professional as possible, never losing sight of the fact that this is a business associate, not your friend, so show some respect.

STEPS

1. **Tell your co-worker you'd like to talk with him in private and ask when a good time for him would be.**

2. **Start with something positive or pay him a compliment. For example, *"I see how hard you've been working these past few weeks."***

3. **Present your issues and suggest solutions.** *"However, I'd like to talk with you about the noise level in our cubicles. When you're talking on the phone, your voice carries to my workstation, making it hard for me to concentrate and do my job. I wanted to discuss it privately and see if we could come up with some solutions together."*

4. **Allow him to respond. Offer a solution when applicable.** For example, *"How about we move our desks around to see if that eliminates the problem and figure out a comfortable volume for our computers?"*

5. **Thank him.** *"I realize this is probably catching you by surprise, and I want you to know how much I appreciate your help."* **Saying thank you gets results;** *"Stop talking so loud, you asshole"* **does not.**

WHILE YOU WERE OUT

If sitting down with your co-worker is too intimidating, try writing him a well-thought-out letter. Choose your words carefully because anything on paper lasts forever, and if needed can turn into evidence.

WHAT YOU CAN WRITE:

> Dear _____,
> It's my hope to keep our office a productive workplace. With that said, I find it hard to do my job when you _____. I'm sure it's not your intention, but it ends up interfering with my work. Would you mind if we tried _____? Thanks for your cooperation.
>
> Sincerely,
>
> _____

BRING IN THE BIG GUNS

If talking to your co-worker and leaving him notes is getting you nowhere, take it up with your boss, supervisor, or human resources. Tread carefully, however, because things are now going on record. Get off on the right foot by showing your boss or HR that your intention is to find a way to work things out. The last thing you want the bigwigs to think is that you're the difficult or annoying co-worker. Try mentioning how different your work styles are and that it would serve you best to have as much separation from your co-worker as possible, especially because your job performance is what's most important to you. Suggest that creating some distance, perhaps by changing floors, cubicles, or desks, will allow you to work at a higher level.

In a Pinch

ANNOYINGCOWORKER.COM

Annoyingcoworker.com is a Web site where people can post information about co-workers and get feedback from the Internet community. Create a post about your co-worker and then the next time everyone is standing around the water cooler, chime in and say, "Hey guys, have you all checked out Annoyingcoworker .com? It's awesome!"

BUBONIC PLAGUE

You know what sucks? Having the plague. Tell your co-worker that you have the bubonic plague and that it probably would be a good idea if he kept his distance. Keep a surgical mask handy.

Dumpipedia

▶ Mickey Rourke was once dumped by the cinema where he worked for getting in a fight with his co-worker.

▶ Careerbuilder.com surveyed 5,700 office workers and discovered that 45 percent of them admitted to falling asleep at work.

▶ The same survey found that 44 percent of men had kissed a co-worker, while only 34 percent of women said the same.

▶ Munchausen at Work is a psychological disorder in which an employee creates a fictional problem at work in order to come up with a solution and gain recognition from superiors.

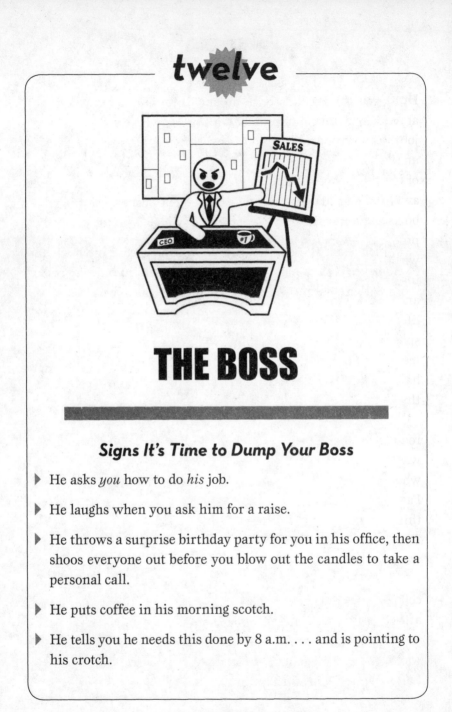

twelve

THE BOSS

Signs It's Time to Dump Your Boss

▶ He asks *you* how to do *his* job.

▶ He laughs when you ask him for a raise.

▶ He throws a surprise birthday party for you in his office, then shoos everyone out before you blow out the candles to take a personal call.

▶ He puts coffee in his morning scotch.

▶ He tells you he needs this done by 8 a.m. . . . and is pointing to his crotch.

Stop Being So Bossy

During the spring of my senior year of college, I worked part-time at a documentary film production company in Manhattan. The job was a lot of grunt work—answering phones, making copies, and delivering packages—but the payback was I got to go on all of the film shoots. While most of my other friends were slaving away at their desk jobs, I was out in the trenches, up to my elbows in filmmaking. I owed it all to Sheila, one of the executive producers, who was my boss and mentor. She went out of her way to make sure I was a part of every step of production: writing treatments, attending pitch meetings, going to film shoots, and, last but not least, editing. Making documentaries was her life, and she was excited to talk about her experiences. I was her sponge, soaking up every minute of it. When she offered to take me out to dinner to celebrate my first day of shooting, I jumped, having never had a boss offer to treat me to a meal. I was beyond thrilled.

What I wasn't thrilled about, however, was how much Sheila required from me outside of work. As it turned out, my mentor was actually quite lonely and in desperate need of a friend. "Hey, what do you say we check out the Film Forum later? There's a Fassbinder retrospective," said Sheila. I couldn't think of anything that I wanted to do less than go sit through a screening of *The Marriage of Maria Braun*—but I was a team player, so I went.

Soon Sheila was calling me to chat both at home and on my cell phone, even when I was working in the next room. Not long after that she was showing up at the office with dog-eared pages in *Time Out* magazine and the *Village Voice* listing things she wanted us to do together. Me, her new best friend. Not only did I already have a best friend (whom I hardly got to see), I had a boyfriend. If any other person in my life made those demands of me, I would have told him to get lost, but this was different. This was my boss. I had no choice—I had to make it work.

From movies to dinner to romantic dates, Sheila was present and accounted for. My boyfriend, who at first was amused by the whole situation, quickly grew tired of it. He liked Sheila. What was not to like? She was interesting, intelligent, and funny. But over time, she took her toll on our relationship. We started bickering more, and most of it was over Sheila. It was time to do something—and fast.

The first thing I knew I had to do was find a way to emotionally separate from Sheila without letting her notice what I was doing. Next, I needed to fill her spare time. But how? And then it dawned on me; what was it that Sheila needed most? Friends! Bingo. I'd make it my priority to introduce her to as many people as possible. The next day, I started fixing her up with everyone I knew. Friends, friends of friends, parents of friends, you name it. I was her pimp: her matchmaker, if you will.

A month later, Project Dump Sheila was declared a total success. When Sheila wasn't going out with one of her new friends, she was spending time researching things to do the next time she did have plans. Concurrently, I was tapering off my after-hours contact with her, changing dinner plans to coffee breaks during work and phone calls to text messages. The best part was that she had no idea what I was doing. Within a month, I got my life back and was able to return to the job I loved without having to worry about being attached at the hip to my boss. For the next few years, I happily made documentaries and loved every minute of it. Sheila and I would catch up when we could, but she had her hands full with her circle of friends and the new part-time production assistant, who shadowed Sheila around the office. Sheila couldn't have been happier—and neither could I.

What I Learned

I wish I had been able to establish boundaries early on with Sheila instead of worrying so much about being seen as a team player. A lot of that had to do with my lack of life and work experience. I now know that if another Sheila comes into my life, I'll have more control of the situation from the start and politely decline outside invitations. While some of us become friends with our co-workers, we must be careful when the person pursuing the friendship is a superior. Not to mention keeping boundaries clear makes it easier to quit, since the relationship has been kept professional.

Bosses know when they hire employees that the day will come when they're going to leave. I was lucky that in the case of Sheila I was able to come up with a plan that shifted her focus away from me and onto other people. But it would have been much easier had we never become friends in the first place. At the very least, I would never have had to suffer through another screening of *The Marriage of Maria Braun*.

Laying the Groundwork

▶ Study your company handbook and make sure that you follow proper protocol.

▶ Refrain from gossiping about your boss in the office.

▶ Don't give your boss any reason to fire you first. Be the one in control of your future, not him.

▶ Take your job performance up a notch. Just because you're about to leave doesn't mean you get to throw away all your current responsibilities. Finish with pride, leaving your boss with a positive memory of how good you were at your job.

▸ If your boss is also your mentor, tread carefully. Start disengaging from him slowly. Choose coffee breaks over lunch. Instead of calling him for advice, call someone else.

▸ Don't tell your co-workers that you've found another job, as people tend to gossip around the office.

▸ Make sure that you have whatever you need backed up or packed away.

▸ Give sufficient notice; two weeks is standard. However, be prepared for your boss to ask you to leave the same day you quit.

▸ Rehearse what you're going to say to your boss. Play out scenarios. If your boss offers to give you more money to stay, will you? Know ahead of time the amount you'd be willing to stay for.

▸ Check all paperwork signed at your current company to make sure you didn't sign a non-competition agreement.

▸ Have another job lined up.

▸ Choose the time and location where you plan to dump your boss. Experts suggest Friday afternoon so that he can have the weekend to sit with his feelings.

▸ Make it your goal to leave on good terms; it's your reputation that's at stake.

Warning: Companies generally frown upon employee jumpers, so think carefully before quitting.

Tip: For those wishing to learn more about your rights in the workplace, check out www.WorkingAmerican.org/

askalawyer/ and ask a lawyer a question. Working America is an affiliate of the AFL-CIO. Its Web site allows you to browse topics ranging from pay and benefits to discrimination and harassment, health and safety, privacy rights, and employment status (which covers firing, layoffs, discipline, workers compensation, and unemployment insurance).

Your Rights in the Workplace

1. A Safe Workplace.

2. Overtime Pay.

3. Equal Pay.

4. Family and Medical Leave.

5. A Workplace without Discrimination.

6. The Right to Join or Form a Union.

7. Unemployment Benefits.

How to Dump 'Em

I QUIT!

You've laid the groundwork; now you're ready to go. Remember, you're not the first employee to move on—and you won't be the last.

STEPS

1. **Let your boss know you have something important to discuss, and ask him when would be a good time to talk. Don't e-mail the request since it's hard to read the tone**

correctly. You don't want your boss to approach the meeting with negative energy.

2. Start with a compliment or something positive. *"I've learned so much from you these past ___ years."*

3. Quit. You don't need to go into great detail, but you should explain enough so that he understands. Be prepared for him not to agree with your decision. Whatever he says, try not to respond in a way that seeks his approval. *"There's no easy way to say this, but it's time for me to move on and try out new work experiences."*

4. Give him adequate time to hire a new person and offer to help train the new employee.

5. Allow your boss to have a reaction—don't try to make him feel better. Let him have his feelings; listen, and try not to be reactive.

6. Thank him for everything. This is important, even if no part of you wants to thank him. It's the right thing to do. Once your boss has accepted your resignation, be sure to go over any unfinished business with him such as unused vacation days, 401(k) issues, unemployment benefits, COBRA, and so on.

LETTER OF RESIGNATION

Dump your boss by submitting a letter of resignation. Choose your words carefully, as the document will most likely stay in your employee file. Make a point of keeping things as positive as possible, expressing gratitude and appreciation. There's no need to get into detailed explanations. If you need your boss to hear you out, make an appointment and do it in person.

Dear _____,

This letter of resignation is to inform you that my last day working at _____ will be on _____. Thank you for the opportunity and experiences.

If you have any questions, please feel free to contact me at _____.

Regards,

_____

BOSS-A-ME-MUCHO

One of the most difficult bosses to dump is the one who has become a friend and mentor. It's even harder if you're leaving to start your own company, one that will rival his. Be as honest as possible without sharing too much information. Think less is more. I spoke to a man who was like a son to his boss, but when he decided to fly the coop and start his own business, he chose not to tell him. Word ended up getting around the office, and his boss found out. The boss was heartbroken, not because his favorite employee and friend was leaving, but because he felt his trust had been betrayed.

Show your boss appreciation by thanking him for being such a great role model. If possible, kill him with kindness. Share with him what you've learned from his guidance. A heartfelt and sincere compliment sets a positive mood and allows for the possibility that he might be happy for you. If he ends up not liking or agreeing with your decision, show empathy, but try your best not to get emotional. This conversation is about work and should remain as professional as possible.

QUIT WITHOUT QUITTING

When quitting is not an option and you have to make things work no matter what, quit without quitting. What on earth am I talking about? How do you dump your boss if you're not quitting? Dump your old ways of dealing with him in favor of a new and improved way. Sit him down, wipe the slate clean, and create a new work environment that both of you can live with.

> WHAT YOU SAY: *"My job means a lot to me. I've sensed that we haven't been connecting, and I was hoping to try and fix that. Is there something I can do differently?"*

By opening the door to communication, you show your boss that you care about your job and are willing to fight for it. Some employees I spoke with resented their bosses for making them do things they felt were above and beyond what their job required them to do. Get rid of that resentment by clearing the air. For example, if your boss is having you pick up his dry cleaning, say, "I'd be happy to pick up your dry cleaning on the way home from work tonight. However, I'd like to take a moment and make sure that I understand my job responsibilities clearly, so that there's no confusion in the future. For instance, I didn't know picking up your dry cleaning was part of my job." You'll be surprised to know how many bosses don't know when they've overstepped their bounds and might end up apologizing for asking you to do things they assumed you didn't mind doing.

BOSS FOR SALE!

Want to dump your boss and get paid for it? Yellojobs.com has come up with a genius idea: "sell your boss." Yellojobs.com is an international recruiting firm that pays you a referral fee if you get someone a job as a result of your posting. Big money, big money!

In a Pinch

SINGING TELEGRAM

Want to make an exit your boss will never forget? Hire a singing telegram to quit for you.

CIRCUS CIRCUS

Tell your boss you've decided to live out your childhood dream of joining the circus. Then juggle your way right out of his office. Don't have anything to juggle? Pretend!

Q. *Why are people so afraid to dump their bosses?*

A. They're afraid of repercussions. They fear that if they try to move on from working with a particular boss, they will hurt their reputation at the company or will, God forbid, end up unemployed. These are, by the way, reasonable concerns.

Q. *What's the biggest mistake people make when they quit?*

A. They burn bridges. Most industries are smaller than you think, and you never know when you might have to work with these people again, or if one of them might become your client in the future.

Q. *How do you know if your boss is getting ready to dump you?*

A. Pay attention to the following warning signs: you received a bad review or were put on probation; you are no longer being consulted on new projects or included in strategic meetings; or your boss has started giving your responsibilities to other people.

Q. *What's the best way to dump your boss?*

A. Don't make it personal, even if it is. If you're transferring bosses or departments, have lunch with your boss and say that you've appreciated everything they have done for you, and you know their guidance will really help as you set out to learn a new skill set. If you're leaving the company, make sure your boss is the first to know, and do everything you can to transition your responsibilities thoroughly so that they have a positive perception of you even as you're walking out the door.

Q. *Is there a time or day of the week when you should dump your boss?*
A. Pick a time when your boss's stress level and workload are as manageable as possible and tell them what you want to talk about so they're prepared. An informal setting like lunch often works best because it allows you to have a conversation that's more personal in nature.

Q. *What's the best way to save the relationship with your boss so that you don't have to dump him?*
A. Sit down with them and have a heart to heart. Tell them how you're feeling and give them the benefit of the doubt. Solicit their feedback regarding how the two of you can improve the relationship and work together more effectively, and then give them a chance to do right by you.

Q. *Why is it so hard to say no to your boss, and what's the best way to do it?*
A. It's hard to say no because people want to be perceived as "can do" employees. Instead of using the dreaded word or saying that you don't have time, ask your boss to help you prioritize your various assignments. You can say something like, "I'd be happy to take care of that, but today I'm researching statistics for the X client's presentation. Which do you think I should do first?"

Q. *Can you teach your boss boundaries, or should you leave that to someone else?*
A. As a general rule, leave it to your boss's manager or spouse. Most boundary offenses—like your boss asking about your personal life, or calling you at home on the weekend—are annoying,

but they aren't deal-breakers. You can, however, set expectations right at the beginning of your employment for how you plan to conduct yourself. For instance, if you don't want to set a precedent for working all the time, allow your boss to see you leaving the office at 6 p.m. and don't answer e-mails from them at midnight.

Q. *If your boss blasts Richard Marx at high decibels, can you say something?*
A. Yes, but be nice about it. Say that you remember the song, but that you're so intent on singing along that you're getting distracted from your work. Just ask if they would mind turning it down a little bit.

Q. *Who's the better boss, Tony Danza or Bruce Springsteen?*
A. Bruce. Tony's a little too in-your-face for me, and Bruce seems to be good at leveraging the contributions of his band members. After all, he's worked with the same people for decades, and he even let one of them star on *The Sopranos*!

DUMPIPEDIA

▶ According to a recent Gallup Management Journal survey, 24 percent of U.S. employees would dump their bosses if given the chance.

▶ Boss's Day is a secular holiday celebrated on October 16 in the United States. It was first registered with the U.S. Chamber of Commerce in 1958 by Patricia Bays Haroski, who was working as a secretary for State Farm Insurance Company in Deerfield, Illinois.

▶ Bruce Springsteen's nickname, "The Boss," originated in the 1960s when he was playing club gigs and had the task of collecting the band's nightly pay and distributing it among his bandmates.

▶ Fifteen million American workers reported that they have bad bosses, and more than 50 million said that they feel pressured to stay with a bad boss because of the weakening economy, according to a recent poll from Lake Research Partners for Working America.

▶ A manager of an Abercrombie & Fitch store in Virginia Beach received a police citation and a fine for refusing to take down risqué photos of models hung on the store's wall. The reason he didn't listen to the cops? His boss told him to display the pictures.

▶ According to the thirteenth annual "Attitudes in the American Workplace" poll conducted by Harris Interactive, 10 percent of U.S. employees say that their company has used e-mail to fire or lay off employees. Another 17 percent said that their bosses used e-mails to avoid face-to-face conversations.

THE CARPOOLER

Signs It's Time to Dump Your Carpooler

▶ He forgets to pick you up.

▶ He reeks of booze at 6:30 a.m.

▶ He keeps whining, "How much farther? Are we almost there?"

▶ He drops his pants and moons other cars.

▶ You're forced to sit on a carpet of pennies, raisins, empty juice boxes, and dog hair.

The Occupancy of
This Vehicle Is High Enough

One summer I was asked to work on a television job that shot on the beautiful island of Kauai. The kicker was that I'd have to work as a local, meaning that I'd have to fly myself there and pay for my own housing. It seemed like a small price to pay, and, as luck would have it, a friend of a pal of mine had a place on the island for rent. Perfect.

What was not so perfect was that the apartment was a good half hour away from where we were filming. I figured I'd find a cheap car to rent and be fine. Not so: what I quickly discovered was that there's no such thing as a cheap car rental in Hawaii. The cost of a car including gas would have equaled the amount of money I'd be making while working there. The good news was that someone at one of the car rental places suggested I check out a local Web site for carpooling. In my mind, carpooling was the same as hitchhiking, which I would never do. However, it seemed to be my only solution, so I sat down at my computer and found my first ride. Oke was a bellhop at the hotel where the crew was staying, which was walking distance to the set. After speaking on the phone, we agreed to a 6:30 a.m. pick-up time. In return for the ride, I'd pay for my share of gas. It seemed like a great plan. But that was before I discovered that 6:30 a.m. Hawaiian time actually meant, "Whenever I feel like it." Oke showed up just after 7:00 a.m., my call time on set. Accompanying him in the car was Pilipo, a valet at the hotel who looked like he'd be more comfortable sleeping on the beach or surfing. They couldn't have been any sweeter or more laid back, making no mention whatsoever of how late they were. I wedged my way in the back next to Keiki, Oke's superstitious golden Labrador.

Keiki only sat in the seat directly behind Oke; if you tried to move her from that side of the car, she'd freak out. If the car happened to make any sudden turns, her paws clung to the seat for dear life.

I made myself as comfortable as possible in the back seat and started breathing through the anxiety of knowing that I was going to be late for my first day of work. Not a good start. The view helped me to relax, and I had no choice but to settle in and enjoy the ride and conversation. For those of you who haven't been to Hawaii, they have a distinct way of speaking that's much more laid back than the rest of Americans, who Hawaiians refer to as "mainlanders." They laughed at my fast-talking New York ways, shaking their heads and saying, "You mainlanders." I never really got the joke but laughed along anyway, not wanting to be left out. I spoke to the guys about showing up on time, but it didn't make a difference. I had no choice but to look into other carpool options. I didn't want to lose the job that I barely started.

Next up was Tiny, who was anything but. Tiny was an electrician at the hotel, and coincidentally lived a few doors down from where I was staying. He was covered in tattoos, head to toe, and drove an old, beat-up white VW bug that looked as though it wouldn't make it to fall. I told him my concerns about timeliness, and he assured me that there wouldn't be a problem. "For seven years, I've left at 6:30 a.m. Trust me, I won't be late."

Tiny was true to his word. At 6:30 a.m. on the nose, he was out front. The problem was he constantly made stops: for snacks, for cigarettes, and for the local ladies. When Tiny saw an attractive woman—or any woman, for that matter—he'd slow the car down, nod his head, and wait for any kind of reaction. And when I say wait, I mean for five, ten, fifteen minutes. He wasn't interested in continuing until he got some kind of acknowledgment. The first week he received zero reactions from any of the girls other than "Keep driving, creep!" But toward the end of the second week, Tiny recognized one of the girls wearing a skimpy bikini top and sarong.

"Aloha, Kaia," said Tiny.

Kaia approached the car, slowly leaned into his window, and gave him the once-over. Then she shot me a look and said, "Who's your friend?"

Tiny replied, "Who? Her? No one—a mainlander—just a carpooler. Trust me, Kaia, she's nowhere near as smokin' hot as you. Mahalo!" And as if that wasn't bad enough, she then walked around to my side of the car and opened my door. Huh? Tiny's tiny car was a two seater. There was a back, but it was suited for a small bag of groceries, nothing more. Both Tiny and Kaia stood there staring at me, totally annoyed. Tiny shot me a look that said, "Get in the back or get out," so I squeezed my way into the tiny crevice and suffered through the next twenty minutes in excruciating pain.

My next carpooler was Ekeka, who worked the grounds at the hotel. I was relieved when he showed up at exactly 6:30 a.m. I wanted to tell him about all the crazy carpoolers I had suffered through, but the moment I got into Ekeka's car he made it clear that he preferred to ride in silence. He said that silence gave him a chance to prepare for the day. That worked for me. Seven minutes later he broke the silence. "It's 6:37 a.m., we are about to pass Popo's Surf Shop." A second later we did. Four minutes later, "It's 6:41 a.m., say hello to Mr. Banana Tree!" And sure enough, we passed a gorgeous fruit tree. I didn't mind his obsessive compulsive behavior—I found it oddly endearing . . . until a few days later, when I asked him if he would stop so I could use the restroom. This he was not prepared for. "It's 6:47 a.m.! We can't stop. We'll be late!" I apologized, saying I would only be a minute, but this only made Ekeka more irritable, so he sped past the next few gas stations at lightning speed. There would be no more stopping, and there would be no more riding with Ekeka.

That put an end to my carpooling in Hawaii. The next day I bit the bullet and rented an outrageously expensive car. When all was said and done, I barely broke even after paying for my bungalow, car, gas, and flight. Would I do it again? Absolutely— have you ever been to Kauai?

What I Learned

Carpooling in Hawaii taught me the importance of going over all the ground rules before stepping a foot in a car. I chose to trust that everything would work itself out instead of asking questions about expectations and car etiquette. That was my mistake. I learned that what is acceptable to me is not necessarily acceptable to someone else. Researching this chapter, I discovered that there are hundreds of Web sites online designed to bring carpoolers together. The most common complaint listed on these sites and from carpoolers whom I spoke to was the lack of proper car rules. When I asked those with long-standing carpools why they didn't implement them now, most said that they were uncomfortable because so much time had passed. But what's worse— having one five-minute conversation or enduring endless suffering? When worded correctly and discussed in the most casual of ways, the rules talk can be an easy and painless conversation to have. Chances are it will be some time before I consider carpooling again, especially since I live in Los Angeles, a city that is so spread out that I would have to carpool in order to get to the other carpoolers.

Laying the Groundwork

▶ Come up with a list of carpool rules and have all the riders agree to it.

▶ Print out the rules and give each carpooler a copy.

▶ Let them know that failure to adhere to the rules is grounds for dismissal.

▶ Decide who in your carpool is going to do the deed and when.

▶ Think about how dumping your carpooler is going to affect your life outside of the car. Be very careful about dumping your boss from a carpool.

Carpool Rules

1. Pick-up time: Discuss proper waiting time. Experts suggest five minutes is enough time to wait.

2. Smoking: Yes or no? Everyone must agree.

3. Radio station: Radio on, or radio off?

4. Stops: None at all, or is the occasional one to the grocery store or dry cleaners okay?

5. Gossiping: Couldn't care less, or strictly forbidden?

6. Cell phones: Okay to use them or never? Most experts agree cell phones should be for emergency use only.

7. Car cleanliness: Got dogs? Be sure to take a vacuum cleaner or lint brush and remove all animal hairs before you pick up fellow riders.

8. Food and drink: No eating or drinking unless agreed upon.

9. Settle all reimbursement costs such as gas or tolls in advance.

10. Devise a backup plan in case of medical or mechanical problems. Make sure that everyone has everyone else's home and cell phone numbers.

11. Seating arrangement: The general rule is taller people in the front, smaller people in the back. Or rotate.

How to Dump 'Em

ROAD RULES
Hopefully by this point, your carpooler has a copy of the car rules, so it won't be a surprise to him when you give him the boot.

WHAT YOU SAY: *"Sorry to be the bearer of bad news, but the carpoolers have all decided that you've broken the rules one too many times, and so we're going to have to let you go. I'm sorry."*

BE PREPARED FOR HIM TO SAY: *"I'll try harder, how about giving me one more chance?"*

FINAL WORD: *"I apologize, but the decision's already been made and it was unanimous."*

RIDE OVER
Usually carpooling is an arrangement based on convenience, not friendship. But even if you've made friends with your carpool, everyone knows that one day, the ride will be over. Call your carpooler and, using as few words as possible, let him know it's the end of the road. Refrain from getting into specifics when possible.

WHAT YOU SAY: *"I'm calling to let you know that we're ending the carpool. This will be the last week. Sorry for the inconvenience."*

BE PREPARED FOR HIM TO SAY: *"Why? What happened?"*

FINAL WORD: *"The biggest thing was that it was too difficult to keep organized. Sorry."*

In a Pinch

STOP PICKING HIM UP

It may not be the nicest way to dump your carpooler, but forgetting to pick him up usually does the trick in no time. Make up whatever excuse you want, from "Whoops, I totally forgot," to "Was that today?" The flakier you are, the better, as carpooling is about being on time. He should dump you pretty quickly.

DUMPIPEDIA

▸ According to AAA, it costs approximately $8,000 per year to operate a mid-size sedan for 15,000 miles.

▸ Slugging is a type of informal carpooling originating in Washington, D.C., whereby drivers can pick up strangers at specific locations and use the HOV lane.

▸ Did you know you that in some cities you can make money carpooling? Take Atlanta's Carpool Rewards program, which allows carpools of three or more to earn gas cards of $20 to $60 each month (depending on the number of riders per car).

▸ Which country in Europe was the first to introduce an HOV lane?
   A. England
   B. The Netherlands
   C. Italy
   D. Germany

The correct answer is B. The Netherlands.
On October 27, 1993, the first HOV lane was opened on the Rijksweg.

part four
HOME
IMPROVEMENTS

fourteen

YOUR FAMILY

Signs It's Time to Dump Your Family

▸ They only call you when they need money—which is at least fifty times a day.

▸ Every Sunday, family night is held in prison.

▸ They leave highway rest stops without you.

▸ Your mother asks you why you can't be more like Chris—and you are Chris.

▸ They make the Jacksons look functional.

Family Unfair

The name Stanley means "meadow that is stony." The reason I know this is because I have a distant relative, Stanley, who, whenever I'd see him at family functions, would quiz me what his name meant—at least two or three times a night. But it wasn't his fondness for quirky games that made Stanley so memorable; it was his enormous height. He stood just over six feet seven inches tall. I was always confused as to how he was related to me, as no one in my family stood anywhere near six feet tall.

Most tall men struggle on the dance floor; however this was not the case with Stanley. He could really dance—and when I say dance, I mean he could move to anything. Waltz, tango, disco, hip hop: you name it, Stanley could do it. In fact, in the early '70s, he sold a videotape that featured Stanley teaching people how to dance by placing vinyl shoe prints on the floor, each with its own number. Stanley danced as he shouted out numbers to people at home, who would then step onto the corresponding cutouts and dance along with him. It was a big hit until some famous dancer copied Stanley and put him out of business.

But the beat went on, and Stanley kept shaking his hips and teaching people how to dance—including me. Stanley taught me how to new wave dance at my cousin Rachel's Duran Duran-themed bat mitzvah. The song was "Notorious," and for the first time, I actually connected with Stanley. Maybe a little too much. Just as he finished showing me a slamming head tilt move, he proudly announced, "That's it, Jodyne! Now you can dance just as good as all the other little black kids." What?! I felt as though someone had kicked me in the gut. I couldn't believe that Stanley would say something so offensive. I come from a long line of progressive liberals who don't tolerate racism. Not my family. Horrified, I rushed over to my father, knowing he would be just as disgusted as I was. I imagined him grabbing the microphone and shaming Stanley in front of the entire family. At the very least, he would give Stanley a good old-fashioned punch to the face.

Instead, my father said, "That's ridiculous! We're Jews! Jews aren't racist! It's just hard to hear him because he's so tall."

It's been over fifteen years since I've seen Stanley. However, he lives on between me and my sisters, like when someone says something politically incorrect, we all look at each other and say, "Look who's pulling a Stanley."

As for my father, he continued refusing to believe that Stanley had a racist bone in his body. However, that changed last fall when my parents were invited over to dinner at Stanley's house. It turns out, as he was giving my folks a tour of the house, he pointed to an extraordinarily high wall in his backyard and said, "The wall had to be that tall so we could keep all the dirty wetbacks from climbing over." My father nearly passed out. He dumped Stanley on the spot, grabbed my mother's hand, and ran out of there without pausing for dinner. It only took him fifteen years to catch on.

What I Learned

My family doesn't do "dumping." The only "D" they practice is denial. My sister once dumped my dad by not talking to him for six months, and my dad convinced himself that it was just because she was busy. But things are different today, at least within my immediate family. If one of us so much as thought about dumping another family member, the rest wouldn't allow it. Planes would be boarded, phones would be dialed—anything and everything would be done to stop it from happening. We may be one hell of a dysfunctional family, but we'll be damn sure that no one dumps anyone from here on out.

But we're the lucky ones. A lot of families don't get along. I spoke with a number of people who haven't communicated with certain family members in years. In some of those cases, I understood their reasons; however, a number of the people couldn't give me a solid reason as to why they were no longer speaking to their children or grandparents or aunts and uncles. They said they hung up the phone or were hung up on and that was it. There was no two-way conversation—just a heated argument in which neither person felt heard. And that's the problem. Dumping your family is complicated, and when you do it, you owe it to your entire family to do it right—that means having a formal conversation or writing them a letter explaining what you want to happen and why.

In the case of Stanley, had I continued seeing him I'm confident I would have said something, as racism or hatred of any kind is something I do not tolerate. My regret is that I looked to my father to stand up and do something instead of doing it myself.

Laying the Groundwork

▶ Write your family member a letter. You don't have to send it, just get all your feelings out on paper.

▶ Clearly define what you wish to have happen when you dump her. Do you want to sever all ties with her permanently, or just for a few months? What about phone calls? Are you open to having one after a month, or not at all? Is an occasional e-mail or card okay? What about family events? Do you both go, or do you take turns? If you both decide to attend, what kind of interaction do you want to have: none at all, or a casual hello? Think of every situation in which you might see your family member at and be very clear about what you would like to have happen should it occur.

▸ Consider a temporary breakup first, which allows everyone time to reflect and potentially fix the problem.

▸ Examine the impact that dumping her is going to have on the rest of your family. For example, if you stop communication with your father and you have a child, you're depriving your child of a relationship with her grandfather.

▸ Decide what you want to hear about the person from other family members. Make sure that after you dump your family member, you tell those affected by your decision what you want or don't want to hear about the dumpee. This will put your other family members at ease—additionally, make sure that you don't put that person in the middle or talk about her negatively.

▸ Define your own personal boundaries. What are you willing or unwilling to do? Since weak boundaries haven't been getting you anywhere, stop saying yes when you mean no. Set your boundaries and make them clear. Whenever possible, offer solutions. Bear in mind that your family most likely has no idea that you have a problem with them. Don't worry. This is your opportunity to gently present your limits. If your mother is nagging you to come to dinner every Friday night, try "I'll come one Friday a month." If your mother still doesn't understand, remember that she doesn't have to agree with your decision; that's why it's your boundary, not hers. There's no need to explain yourself here. It's not up to you to take care of her feelings. If you're not yet sure what your boundaries are, sit still for a minute. Ask your body how it feels when your family member does something that bothers you. Go through a list if you need to. Does something make your stomach turn? There's your answer. That's where you need to draw a boundary.

▶ Enforce the boundaries. Let's say you have a family member who keeps calling to tell you how much she doesn't like what you're doing with your life. Let her know that you don't wish to discuss this issue with her; if she continues to disrespect you, tell her that the next time it happens, you're going to hang up the phone. Then, if it happens again, point out what she's doing; if she continues to disrespect you, announce that "I'm hanging up now," then put the phone down. At this point, you're not helping anyone by staying on the line. Enforcing boundaries is your responsibility; it's going to feel weird at first, but eventually you'll feel empowered because you're honoring yourself. Saying no is one of the most powerful boundaries there is; it sends a clear message that you exist apart from your family member and that you're the one in control of your life, not her.

Tip: Try coming up with a handy list of fallback answers, making sure that you're saying no very clearly. For instance, if your father asks you to help your sister go shopping for bridal dresses, you say, "I'm sorry, I already have plans." If you're pressed with a "What's more important than helping your sister?" you might say, "I have plans. It doesn't mean that I don't love my sister." Make sure that your "no" is firm.

▶ Learn additional ways to emotionally distance yourself from your family, such as letting the phone go to voicemail and using caller ID. Be less available to your toxic family member. This is not about avoiding, it's about learning to not always say yes.

▶ Practice. This is a process, so allow time to take on your new role, and for your family members to adjust to it.

Tip: Breaking up with a family member is about making positive changes in your life, not about hurting her feelings or acting out of rage. Don't even consider dumping anyone in your family until you can discuss things in a calm and collected voice. Hanging up on someone or refusing to talk to her doesn't address the issue and leaves the situation murky and unclear. Your goal should be to be as clear and honest with your family member as possible so that there's no room for misunderstanding. This creates less stress for both of you, and no one has to guess what she did wrong.

How to Dump 'Em

THERAPISTS DO IT BETTER

Making the decision to dump your family is difficult and sometimes impossible to do on your own, especially while trying to protect other family members (including your spouse or children). This is where a good therapist can really make a difference. Not only will she be able to help you process your reasons for wanting to dump your family member, she can also help to facilitate the actual conversation in a safe environment. Having a neutral third-party professional involved allows every voice to be heard and keeps things on course. A good therapist also provides emotional comfort and encouragement.

SEE U-HAUL LATER

Sometimes the only way to dump your family is to physically move away. This doesn't have to be a permanent move, but for those of you whose family has threatened your emotional or physical safety—or who come from a family that lacks boundaries and makes you feel suffocated—a solid choice is to get as far away from them as possible. I spoke to a woman who was raised by an overbearing mother—no matter where she moved in town, her mother showed up unannounced. She tried a number of small moves over the years, but her mother continued to make her presence known in this woman's life. Finally, at the age of thirty, she dumped her mother by moving across the country. She didn't tell her mother where she had moved, but told her that she'd contact her once she was settled. It drove her mother crazy—but three months later, the daughter called. For the first time in her life, she had the relationship she had always wanted with her mother. That was over ten years ago, and she's never been happier, because she's finally living the life she wants.

Tip: A physical separation allows for self-reflection and, in time, can create a healthier relationship dynamic, making for an easier transition should you wish to move back in the future.

WHAT YOU SAY: *"I've decided to move away in order to create some space between us, allowing for some much needed perspective on our relationship. I will call you when I am ready."*

BE PREPARED FOR HER TO SAY: *"Huh? What does that mean?"*

FINAL WORD: *"It means that I'm moving away in order to make some changes in my relationship with you and to gather my thoughts. It doesn't mean that I don't care for you or love you; it just means that I need things to change, and that the change must begin with me."*

FAMILY UNTIES

When you've exhausted your options and the only way to move forward is by severing ties with your family, take plenty of time and prepare yourself. Know exactly what you want to say and have happen before having the conversation.

Warning: Don't approach this conversation if you still have an emotional charge.

STEPS

1. Give your family member the heads-up that you'd like to have a private conversation with her about the two of you. If she asks what's up, tell her that you've been thinking a lot about your relationship and that you'd like to talk to her when she's ready and open to discussing it. Let her think that you're the one with the problem; just avoid getting into the conversation in that moment, as adrenaline is usually high, and it usually helps for the other person to have some time to sit with things.

2. Sit down with or call your relative and tell her what your issues are, being sure to cite specific examples. This conversation is not about attacking your family member; you've already made the decision to dump her, so stick to listing your reasons. Word things in a way that doesn't blame her but instead describes things she says or does that make you uncomfortable.

3. Tell her what you want to have happen. No communication for six months? One year? Do you want the two of you to have some time apart to think about how to have a better relationship? Would you prefer never to see her again? Have a phone call in a year? Be specific.

4. Allow her to respond. Stay calm and focused. When people are hurt, they tend to attack, so be prepared and make every effort not to engage in a fight. Listen and

refrain from more dialogue unless you absolutely feel that it's warranted.

5. Tie up loose ends. If there are family functions to attend (such as weddings or holidays), go over who will go and what kind of interaction you'd like to have if you see her there (or any other place, for that matter). The point of this conversation is not to leave anything unclear or murky, so cover all your bases.

6. End the conversation. A common mistake people make is to continue talking long after your point has been made. Usually it's nerves. Do your best at exiting the conversation as soon as possible, preferably while still on a good note. Depending on the situation, you might thank her for understanding or apologize if her feelings are hurt. Make it a point not to hang up on her.

In a Pinch

LOOK WHO'S NOT TALKING

Tell your family that you've decided to give your voice box a rest until further notice and see how they handle it. Provide them with pens and paper. The hope is that eventually they will beg you to start talking about what's wrong and how they can fix it. When this happens, use your pen and write a note explaining what needs to change in order for you to start speaking again.

Q&A
Sarah Silverman
EMMY AWARD-WINNING COMEDIENNE AND STAR
OF *THE SARAH SILVERMAN PROGRAM.*
She's also my sister.

Q. *Do you remember the first time you were dumped?*
A. Yes!! I was in 3rd grade, and Eric Arnold power-walked toward me with Tom Wheeler next to him. I saw him coming toward me and smiled. He never slowed down—he just fast-walked right by me and as he passed he barely tilted his head my way and said, "You're dumped," and continued on. It was awesome.

Q. *Why do you think the word "dump" is so funny?*
A. Well, it has the classic comedy "P" sound. And then just to be able to extract a "P" sound out of dump is ironic—in the basest possible way.

Q. *What do you, Sarah Silverman, think is the best way to dump a family member?*
A. Well, I've been meaning to talk to you, Jodyne. . . . Wow, a family member. Hm. You'd probably just have to kill them.

Q. *Do you think that when our sister Susie moved her family to Israel that she was trying to dump us?*
A. I like to think of it as moving thousands of miles toward us— the long way around.

Q. *What are the signs that you've been dumped by your family?*
A. Probably a constant unavailability—never picking up calls— always calling back when they know you're not available.

Q. *Have you ever wanted to dump me? Or have you tried, and I was too thick to notice?*
A. No!! Well, not yet.

Q. *Just so I know, should I wish to dump you one day, how would you like me to do it?*
A. You'd probably have to fake your death to get rid of me.

▶ In 1587, Elizabeth I dumped her cousin Mary, Queen of Scots, by condemning her to death after discovering that Mary had been researching the effects of heavy metal poisoning on family ties.

▶ *Irreconcilable Differences* is a 1984 movie starring Drew Barrymore as a little girl who wants to dump her parents by divorcing them.

▶ Family Day is a public holiday in South Africa, Australia, and Canada. It was established to allow workers to take the day off and be with their families.

▶ The custom of honoring mothers goes back at least as far as seventeenth-century England, which continues to celebrate Mothering Sunday.

▶ During "Family Hour," programs of general interest to the family are broadcast. What block of time is considered family hour?
   A. 8:00 p.m.–11:00 p.m.
   B. 7:00 p.m.–10:00 p.m.
   C. 6:00 p.m.–9:00 p.m.

The answer is C. 6:00 p.m.–9:00 p.m.

fifteen

THE NANNY/BABYSITTER

Signs It's Time to Dump Your Nanny/Babysitter

▶ She asks for a flat-screen TV with HBO for her room.

▶ She didn't pick up your kids because she needed a quiet afternoon at home . . . your home.

▶ You come home just in time to find her boyfriend sneaking out the back door half-naked.

▶ She tells you that "visiting hours" are over and won't let you see your kids.

▶ She makes trail mix with your prescription pills.

The Final Time Out

Okay, so I haven't exactly had to hire a nanny, but I have had to fire one. Let me explain. My best friend, Leslie, and I pimp each other out, doing things the other one doesn't want to do—like returning clothing to Barneys without a receipt, switching cell phone providers, or firing nannies. Leslie, who has two very sweet children, made the mistake of hiring one awful nanny. Maria was hired because she had a glowing recommendation from her previous employer, and because Leslie's kids (eight months and two years old) took to her immediately. I fell for her too, which says a lot, since I've been known to be a tad judgmental. Maria was kind, soft-spoken, and a natural giver who loved to sing. She sang like an angel. All Maria had to do was walk into a room and Leslie's younger daughter, Sophia, would light up. Jealous of this, I'm embarrassed to admit, I spent more than one occasion entering and re-entering a room, hoping to get that same reaction.

Maria didn't strike us as the kind of person who has a dark side. She had always been gentle and sweet to everyone, so it came as a total shock when Leslie's neighbor dropped by to inform her that the soft-spoken Maria whom we had all come to love had turned into the neighborhood Latina Norma Rae, preaching to the other nannies on the block to work less, demand more money, and insist on additional days off. She even stole construction paper and glitter glue from Leslie's kids to make posters.

Hesitant to dump Maria because the kids loved her, Leslie decided to put up with it—but not for long. As time went on, Leslie's older daughter, Anabelle, started talking, and we were all introduced to her strong, dynamic, highly entertaining personality. Maria wasn't exactly thrilled to meet the new Anabelle. She started to withdraw from Anabelle more and more. When

Anabelle followed Maria around the house, Maria got irritated, shooing her away. It was heartbreaking to watch little Anabelle excitedly run to Maria and present her with a flower—only to get the cold shoulder. It became crystal clear that Maria loved babies, but not kids—especially not kids who could talk. That was the final straw; Maria would have to be dumped immediately. Leslie could tolerate Maria's neighborhood shenanigans, but she would not watch her favor one child over the other. The next day she sat Maria down and asked her to leave. Maria's response? "No, thank you. I'm good." Leslie, not sure that Maria had understood, asked her again. To which Maria replied, "I will stay. Thank you." Then she got up, hugged Leslie, and sang her way out of the room. Leslie had no idea what had just happened.

That's when I got the call. It's funny how easy it is for me to spring into action on someone else's behalf. Fifteen minutes later, I was handing Maria her severance pay and offering to help pack her bags and give her a ride home. There was no misunderstanding this time. She grabbed the check from my hand, stormed out of the room, and in five minutes she was packed and out of the house. She refused my ride, opting instead to lug her giant black duffle bag up the street, singing her way to the nearest bus stop. Mission complete.

What I Learned

It's not an easy task finding the right nanny for one's kids. I watched Leslie interview and test out several nannies before finally choosing Maria. There was a nanny who Leslie loved, but her kids didn't, so it was back to the drawing board. I learned from Leslie's mistake just how important it is to come up with questions and scenarios for every situation possible and to clearly go over everything before offering your nanny the job. It never occurred to Leslie to ask Maria how she felt about kids; she just assumed that since she loved babies, she would naturally love kids—something she could have found out easily if she had asked Maria about her experience with kids. As it turned out, Maria had none. She had only worked with babies.

The majority of parents I spoke to made it a point to go over everything with their nannies before they started. However, when it came time to speak up or dump their nanny, a large number of them found it too difficult. A few expressed how they didn't want to rock the boat for fear their nanny would take out her feelings on the kids. Others, especially those living in cities, said they would rather put up with a mediocre nanny instead of looking for another one. They felt it was nearly impossible to find the perfect nanny.

I now know that if I ever have to hire a nanny, I will not only go over everything thoroughly, but I will make it a point of scheduling check-ins. Check-ins are a great way of staying connected with your nanny and in turn staying connected with your kids. A surprisingly high number of nannies that I interviewed revealed how underappreciated they felt. I'm going to go out of my way if I have a nanny to make her feel as welcome in my home as possible and, when appropriate, I'll be sure to give her a bonus, because a happy nanny means a happier child.

Laying the Groundwork

▶ Make sure your expectations are clearly established.

▶ Write down your list of reasons for wanting to dump your nanny or babysitter.

▶ Give her at least one warning. Explain specifically what problems you're having, letting her know that if things don't change, her job is at risk.

▶ Study any contracts with the nanny/babysitter. Consult a lawyer if needed.

▶ If you went through an agency, speak to the agency about how to handle termination.

▶ Decide on severance pay. The general rule of thumb regarding severance pay is a week's salary for every year she worked for you.

▶ Take inventory of all things the nanny/babysitter still has in her possession.

▶ Rehearse what you're going to say.

▶ Prepare what you're going to say to your children after the nanny/babysitter has been fired.

▶ Have another nanny lined up. Check out www.Nanny Network.com, www.Nannies4Hire.com, or www.SitterCity .com.

▶ If appropriate, write a letter of recommendation before you fire her.

▶ Have your checklist ready of people to call after you dump your nanny/babysitter, so they know not to release your child to her.

Sample Checklist of People to Call After You Dump Your Nanny

1. School.

2. Doorman.

3. Security Guard.

4. Extracurricular Instructors: Your Child's Tae Kwon Do Sensei, Ballet Teacher, Soccer Coach, and So Forth.

5. Parents of Your Children's Friends.

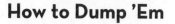

How to Dump 'Em

TIME FOR YOU TO (BABY)SIT THIS ONE OUT
Your kids come first, so don't dump your nanny/babysitter while they're at home. The last thing you want is for your kids to see you fire their favorite caretaker.

STEPS

1. **Sit down with your nanny/babysitter. Show compassion, but be firm. The decision's been made. It's no longer up for discussion.**

2. **Start with a compliment or something positive.** *"My kids have really loved the way that you sing them to sleep."*

3. **Bring to her attention the times when you've given her prior notice.** *"As I have pointed out on several occasions, I've needed you to _____."*

4. **Stress the importance of the issue.** *"These are my children and it is important that _____."*

5. **Dump her and give her severance pay.** *"Unfortunately, because things haven't changed, I'm going to have to let you go. Here's an envelope with two weeks' pay."* **If appropriate,** *"I have included a letter of recommendation as well."*

6. **Allow her to respond. Be sure to stick to your guns.** If she mentions bills to be paid or other issues that may tap into your guilt, express compassion, but try your best not to engage in more conversation.

7. **Discuss how she wishes to say good-bye to your children.** Come back tomorrow? Another day?

8. **Thank her.**

MONEY'S TIGHT

Finances are a huge reason why people can't afford a nanny. When money gets in the way, it's time to jettison the nanny.

> WHAT YOU SAY: *"Things are tough for us financially right now, which means that unfortunately we're going to have to let you go. I'm so sorry for any inconvenience. [When appropriate] I've taken the liberty of writing you a letter of recommendation. Thanks for everything."*

STAY-AT-HOME PARENT

Kids grow up fast. An easy way to dump your nanny is to tell her that you don't want to miss a single minute of it and want to be a full-time parent. Then flatter her with compliments and ask for tips and suggestions.

THE IN-LAWS

Tell your nanny/babysitter that your in-laws are moving in with you and have offered to take care of your children. Mention how much your kids love them.

In a Pinch

IT'S NOT ME! IT'S MY KIDS!

You're not firing them, your kids are! Tell your nanny/babysitter that your children are having a hard time adjusting to her. Come up with a reason, such as "They still can't seem to let go of their old nanny," "You know kids, they can be so fickle sometimes," or "My kids are so obsessed these days with all the English nannies in movies like *Mary Poppins* and *Nanny McPhee* that they insist I hire one with an English accent. How are you with accents?"

SUPERNANNY

Sit your nanny down and watch a marathon of *Supernanny*, the TV show where nannies visit people's homes, observe families in action, and then help them restore order. Tell your nanny how fun it would be to be on television and that you're going to write to the producers of the show. Then a few weeks later come home waving an envelope in the air and tell her that you've been chosen to be on the show! Uh-oh. I guess that means she won't be needed anymore—sorry!

Q. *What are the most common reasons that people want to dump their nanny?*

A. The decision to let your nanny go is never easy and there are many different reasons why a family may feel it is necessary to make this change. The most common reason is the simple fact that the family's needs have changed; many times a nanny is hired for a certain period of time, such as infancy or during the toddler years. Some families will no longer need the help of a nanny when their children begin to attend school. Other families will keep a nanny until their children start high school or until they simply do not need a nanny anymore. On the other hand, there are also situations in which the reasons for the change are less desirable. One mother, for example, found that her nanny's personality did not mesh with her own. Another mother said that her nanny refused to follow the schedule she had prepared for the nanny and her children. Before making a change, be sure to assess whether or not the problem is behavioral. Although we might wish it, nannies are not mind readers! If you have particular ways of doing things in your home, let the nanny know. Although you may think that your preferences are common practice, it may have been different in their previous positions. In most cases, an attempt should be made to communicate with the nanny and to give them an opportunity to correct the behavior. If this is not possible, or if the changes are not made to your satisfaction, it may be time for a change.

Q. *What's the best way to dump a nanny?*
A. The best way to let a nanny go is to be kind and gracious. Sitting down and discussing the reasoning behind the decision is preferred. If the change is due to the natural evolution of the family structure—such as the children starting school or the family having grown out of the need for a nanny—this conversation should be fairly simple. After explaining the situation, express your appreciation for their dedicated service and assure them that they will always be a dear friend to the family and to the children. Many parents will invite former caregivers to family events such as bar mitzvahs or birthday parties. If the nanny was a good employee and caregiver to your children, it is also important to give them a reference letter for future employment. Some families will also provide a severance package to the nanny; a typical severance package is two weeks' pay. Severance pay is not expected for babysitters or part-time nannies. Letting a nanny go when the reason for the change is neither natural nor mutual is often more difficult, and these are the conversations that parents dread the most. The best way to handle these situations is to be honest; if you can't stand their personality, let them know that you feel the long-term personality fit is not the best. If the nanny did not follow your directions, let them know that you were dissatisfied with their ability to take direction and follow through. The nanny will appreciate your honesty and the helpful criticism will be useful in their next position. When firing a nanny, always consult with your attorney to make sure that you are protected from any potential discrimination claims.

Q. *What's the most outrageous story you've heard about someone dumping a nanny?*

A. Our agency once heard of a celebrity employer letting a nanny go in the middle of the night. All of a sudden, the assistant knocked at the nanny's door and let her know that her services were no longer required. She was told to pack her things and leave at 3:00 a.m.

Q. *Is there a wrong way to dump a nanny?*

A. Yes. After a nanny has worked for a period of time with a family, there are bonds that have been created—especially with the children. It is important to let the nanny know why the decision has been made and to treat them kindly and with respect. It is also important to involve the children in the process of saying good-bye and to make the parting a happy one.

Q. *What's the best way to ask a nanny to stop prancing around the house wearing her Daisy Dukes?*

A. As Plato once said, "The beginning is the most important part of the work." One could say the same about hiring a nanny. It is important when hiring a new nanny that the family is very clear in the beginning about the expectations and requirements of the position. Appropriate work attire is a topic that should be addressed, and clear guidelines should be established before the nanny begins working.

Q. *How should a parent deal with a nanny if she suspects that the nanny is stealing?*

A. A nanny must be an individual of integrity and of high moral character. If a parent strongly suspects and/or is presented with evidence that their nanny is stealing, the family should let the nanny go immediately. This behavior is illegal and is unacceptable. In a situation where an item has been stolen and several staff members could be responsible, an effort should be made to objectively investigate the situation. However, be careful not to accuse your nanny of stealing if you do not have concrete evidence. One of our clients came home one night to find a valuable necklace missing. She instantly assumed the nanny was responsible and angrily accused the nanny of stealing; the next day, she found the necklace and realized she had simply misplaced it. Unfortunately, by this time the damage had already been done, and the nanny no longer felt comfortable working in the home. The family lost an amazing nanny by jumping to conclusions.

Q. *How do you politely ask a nanny to mother less and nanny more?*
A. Open communication between the parents and the nanny is crucial in a good family/nanny relationship. It is important that the nanny respect the parents and the way in which they would prefer their children are raised. A professional nanny will listen to the parents and put their wishes into practice with their children in matters such as routine and discipline. If you feel that your nanny is trying to take over and you don't like it, speak up and be direct. Take control of the situation by becoming more involved in the day-to-day decisions. Try creating a schedule for your nanny and children or begin checking in throughout the day. Be open with your nanny if you feel that she is being too overbearing. Remember, you are the parent and the nanny is your employee. Be open to observations and suggestions by your nanny, but always remember that you have the right to dictate exactly how your children are cared for.

Q. *Who termed the word "manny"?*
A. The first ever mention of the word "manny" was used in an article in the *Washington Post* in 1986. Before that time, TV's classic *Family Affair* featured a male nanny, Mr. French. Recently, mannies have been gaining popularity and attention in the press

due to celebrities such as Britney Spears hiring a manny for her children.

Q. *What do you think is the most common misconception people have about nannies?*
A. Unfortunately, the media has portrayed nannies as seductive bombshells looking for their next conquest. This stereotype has not been helped by highly publicized celebrity affairs with nannies such as Jude Law's, whose affair with his own nanny was put on public display. On an episode of *Desperate Housewives*, Lynette decided to fire her nanny because she felt she was too attractive. This is a stereotype that nannies must fight. Nannies are caregivers because working with children is their passion. The idea that there are a large number of nannies that are pining away after their employers is absurd. And most nannies don't look like Scarlett Johansson in the *Nanny Diaries*. To a professional nanny this is their calling, not just a job, and the desirability of the parents is the last thing on their mind.

Q. *Who is your favorite TV/film nanny and why?*
A. I hate to sound cliché, but Marry Poppins is to this day my all-time favorite. A nanny who can clean in a snap, make medicine go down like a spoonful of sugar, and encourage the children to use their imagination is worth her weight in gold.

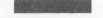

DUMPIPEDIA

▶ Britney Spears dumped her nanny when her son fell out of his highchair.

▶ Robin Williams and Ethan Hawke both married their children's nannies.

▶ Nanny also means a female goat.

▶ Fran Drescher, star of *The Nanny*, had her first break in what movie?
  A. *Animal House*
  B. *Saturday Night Fever*
  C. *This Is Spinal Tap*
  D. *When Harry Met Sally*

▶ Julia Roberts wished her nanny, Marva, a "happy birthday" from the Academy Awards.

The correct answer is B. Saturday Night Fever.
Fran played the character Connie.

sixteen

THE HOUSEKEEPER

Signs It's Time to Dump Your Housekeeper

▶ She tells you that scrubbing your bathtub and shower is "not my thing."

▶ You have to clean up after her.

▶ She creates her own wish list on your TiVo.

▶ She hands you a list of products she needs from the store— and it includes cosmetics and cookies.

▶ You come home to find her sleeping in your bed and cradling your phone.

Cleaning House

Waiting for Betty to show up was like waiting for a blind date to arrive. I was excited, anxious, nervous—you name it, I felt it. I had never had a cleaning woman before, and so had no idea of what to expect. Would she like me? Would I like her? I hoped so; after all, I'd spent the last four hours scrubbing my apartment so that she wouldn't think I was some kind of pig. How would we discuss payment? She was taking the bus to my apartment. Was I supposed to offer her a ride home? My head was spinning and I had the nervous sweats.

And then my buzzer rang. I jumped, making sure to check my hair and my breath in the mirror. I opened the door and there she was, all five feet two inches of her, holding a plate of cookies, crumbs on the front of her blouse—most likely from eating one moments before she rang the buzzer. "I hope you like chocolate chip," chimed a happy Betty as she marched past me and to the kitchen, where she set the plate on the counter before opening the refrigerator. "Oh, good, you have milk. Want a glass?" Who was this woman? She's amazing. "Yes, please. Thanks!" Betty poured me a glass of milk, set it in front of me, and made her way into my cleaning closet, lifting up bottles, examining labels, nodding her head at some, shaking it at others. "What about gloves?" she asked. I froze.

"Gloves? Oh. I don't have gloves. I'm sorry. I should have asked you on the phone what you needed," I said.

She laughed and waved her hand, saying, "I'm just kidding you. I brought my own." She's funny. Nice. At the end of the day I wrote her a check. She took it and said, "See you next Monday!" and then off she went.

Betty was the best—a total character. Some days she'd bring cookies, other times leftover pot roast, another time it was banana bread. She never showed up without some kind of a gift or surprise. And her stories always entertained me, whether they were about her deadbeat husband, her sister with narcolepsy, or her daughter, who had a habit of painting moustaches on her classmates using a sharpie. There was always something going on in her life that provided me with laughter.

But with each story came a little less professionalism on her end. What started as casual chatter while mopping the floor morphed into her kicking off her shoes, plopping down on my couch, smacking the bottom cushion, and motioning for me to join her. "Well? What are you waiting for? Sit. You're the writer, write this," and she'd launch into another story. Although I was still interested, I was more interested in having her clean my house.

Before I knew what was happening, she had put paper towels in my right hand and a bottle of Windex in the other, and suddenly I was cleaning with her. The problem was that even with my help, the quality of her work was suffering. Her eyes were focusing more on me than on my filthy sink, greasy floor, or dirty laundry basket, which were often overlooked. I couldn't gather the courage to say something to her directly, so I decided that I would give her a key to my apartment and make a point of not being there when she showed up.

Unfortunately, it didn't help. The showers remained filthy, the new duster that she had specifically asked for was still unopened, and I had to leave notes to remind her to clean the fridge. I finally worked up the courage to say something, which, I admit, was a bit passive aggressive. "Betty, is everything okay? I've noticed that you haven't been scrubbing the bathroom lately."

She responded with a giggle. "You must be blind, Miss Jodyne." That's my Betty: a real jokester.

By this point, my friends insisted that I fire her, but I couldn't—partly because I thought she would laugh at me. The weeks continued to go by, with very little getting clean. And then, one day I received a phone call from Betty telling me she had to go to Guatemala for a few months to help her mother. Her good friend, Rosie, would fill in for her while she was away. "Don't worry, Miss Jodyne. I'll be back soon."

The following week, Rosie arrived, and although she came without cookies or a pot roast, and had nothing like Betty's engaging personality, she was unbelievable. I cried like a baby after the first time she cleaned my apartment. The woman left no surface untouched. Every floor and cabinet sparkled, the faucets and showers gleamed, and the windows were so clean I could see my reflection in the panes of glass. And did she organize? Like nobody's business. She was the dream housekeeper, and before long, I found myself praying that Betty would not return from Central America.

Three months later, the dreaded call came; Betty was back. It was time to say adios to Rosie. The following Monday, Betty showed up bearing presents from Central America. We spent the day talking about her trip, her mother, and her cousins. Then she took her check and left, never having touched a sponge or a mop. I couldn't stop daydreaming about Rosie and the way she cleaned my bathroom, how she organized the paperwork on my desk, and the cute way she folded my socks. I only wished I had gotten one more week with her, because she was about to alphabetize my kitchen pantry.

Betty's next visit wasn't any better. She must have decided to stop getting on chairs and stepladders while she was away, which meant that everything higher than five feet two inches off the ground remained dirty. That was it. I'd had it; I was ready to fire her. The following Monday, as soon as she opened the door, I asked her to take a seat. Just as I was about to begin, Betty beat me to the punch. "Oh, listen to this. Rosie? Some friend—would you believe that little backstabber stole half my clients? After I helped her for all those months, this is how she repays me? Some people." Ugh! I couldn't do it now. How could I fire her after that? I froze, staring into her dark brown eyes.

The two of us spent the next three hours cleaning. Well actually it was more like I cleaned and she watched. In the middle of scrubbing the bathtub, I came up with an idea. I'm not saying it was a great idea, but it was an idea. I would rehire Rosie while still keeping Betty. I'd have Rosie come later in the week. This way, no one would have to be fired. Sure, it would cost more, having two housekeepers, but at least Betty's feelings wouldn't get hurt.

The next week, Rosie cleaned my apartment. The plan was working perfectly—until two weeks later, when I came home from work and found Rosie and Betty both sitting on my couch, arms crossed, pissed. Betty did the talking. "Really?"

To which I hesitantly said, "Yes?"

They stood up, grabbed their bags, and headed for the door. "Looks like someone needs to find herself a new housekeeper," said Betty. And like that, my plan backfired. It was back to cleaning my own apartment . . . until my phone rang. It was Rosie, whispering into the phone that she wanted back in. Three days later, my entire kitchen pantry was alphabetized.

What I Learned

For starters, don't hire two housekeepers. Next, don't grab a roll of paper towels and start cleaning with your housekeeper. Keep your private life to yourself and don't open the door to hers. Avoid making her feel so comfortable that she has no problem kicking off her shoes, resting on your couch, or bringing her kids over so you can babysit them while she cleans. You've got to establish boundaries right away. Write them down if you need to; just make sure that your housekeeper knows exactly what your expectations are. Then walk away and let her work. The sooner that you communicate your needs, the easier it will be for her to meet them. And remember to compliment your housekeeper; it's not fun to clean homes, and it's always nice to have someone appreciate your hard work.

Laying the Groundwork

▶ Go over what you want your housekeeper to do each visit— vacuum, dust, scrub the bathroom—it may be obvious to you, but not to her.

▶ If she's not completing her assigned tasks, make a note of this along with any other things that aren't working for you, then sit her down and go over the list, pointing out what she missed.

▶ Give her a few warnings, making sure that she understands that if she doesn't do what you're asking, she'll be let go.

▶ Write a list of all the outstanding items still in her possession and ask to have them back. Remember that bitter cold day last winter when your housekeeper borrowed your shearling coat? Ask for it back. Your favorite hand cream from Paris—get it back! Same goes for all rugs, sheets, clothes, or any other personal belongings that you may or may not know about.

▶ Give her some kind of severance pay.

▶ When appropriate, offer to write her a letter of recommendation.

- Find a new housekeeper. Ask for referrals or check out www .HireHousekeepers.com or www.HousekeeperHelp.com.

- Change the locks and security codes to your house. It's better to be safe than sorry.

Warning: Did you know there are no industry standards governing the cleaning industry? This means that anyone can advertise her housekeeping services and show up at your house.

How to Dump 'Em

CLEANING HOUSE

Hopefully by this point, you've laid the groundwork, so it won't come as a big surprise to your housekeeper when you tell her that things haven't been working out. Remember to keep the conversation to as few words as possible. Getting emotional is not going to help either one of you. This conversation is not about getting your housekeeper to understand you or think you are a good person. This is business, so keep it that way.

STEPS

1. **Ask her to take a seat.**

2. **Start with a compliment.** *"I see how hard you work each week."*

3. **Mention the warnings you have given her.** *"As I pointed out, I've been unhappy with your work these past few months."*

4. **Dump her.** *"Because the tasks I have needed you to do don't seem to be getting done, I'm letting you go."*

5. **Let her respond. She might ask for a second chance. Cut this off swiftly.** *"I'm sorry, that's just not possible."*

6. **Offer her some severance pay and a letter of recommendation.**

7. **Thank her.**

STRAPPED FOR CASH

For most people, having a housekeeper is a luxury. If the money is not coming in, neither should the housekeeper.

WHAT YOU SAY: *"I'm so sorry, but cash is tight right now, so I'm going to have to let you go."*

BE PREPARED FOR HER TO SAY: *"I'll work for less money."*

FINAL WORD: *"That's very kind of you, but I wouldn't be comfortable with that. Thank you for offering."*

HOME IMPROVEMENT

Anyone who's ever renovated a house knows how time-consuming it is. Dump your housekeeper by telling her that you've decided to make some big changes to your house. Go ahead and show her how excited you are while stressing how overwhelmed you are since the whole process will take at least ten months to a year to complete. Mention the mess it will create, especially because you're taking down walls, replacing the plumbing, and re-wiring the entire house.

ONE MAN'S TRASH IS ANOTHER MAN'S TREASURE

When my sister moved, she took that opportunity to let her housekeeper go. While it's true she had some problems with her housekeeper, none of them had anything to do with her cleaning ability. I called my friend Leslie, who had been looking for a housekeeper, and gave her this woman's number. Leslie ended up loving her, and she's been cleaning Leslie's house ever since. So why not set your housekeeper up with someone else? You just might be doing her a favor.

In a Pinch

I'M MOVING

Tell your housekeeper that you're packing it up and moving out of town, which means that you won't be needing her anymore.

CUJO

Tell your housekeeper that you bought a pit bull to protect the house, and while he's just the sweetest little pit bull around the family, he's really aggressive with outsiders. In just a few days, he's already responsible for thirteen stitches. Ouch!

Q&A
Aggie Mackenzie
CO-HOST OF THE BBC AMERICA TELEVISION SHOW
HOW CLEAN IS YOUR HOUSE?, **AS WELL AS CO-AUTHOR**
OF THE BOOK OF THE SAME NAME.
www.aggiemackenzie.co.uk

Q. *How do you dump your housekeeper?*
A. White lies every time—your circumstances have changed: less money, getting an *au pair*, whatever it takes.

Q. *What can you do if you suspect that your favorite housekeeper is getting ready to dump you?*
A. Take her out to lunch and re-establish the relationship.

Q. *What's the polite way to tell your housekeeper that she's missed a spot?*
A. Just be very straightforward about it!

Q. *Is there one cleaning tip every housekeeper should know—but most likely doesn't?*
A. That it is lovely to be pleasantly surprised by the housekeeper doing something beyond their remit—like sorting out the linen cupboard, for instance. It almost doesn't matter that the bathroom sink isn't quite up to scratch!

Q. *What are the rules about a housekeeper breaking things?*
A. It's too bad, really—that's the risk you have to take. If it becomes a habit, time to let her go!

Q. *What's the biggest mistake people make with their housekeepers?*
A. Not treating that person as a fellow human being.

Q. *How do you tell your housekeeper that her work isn't up to par?*
A. Be gentle but firm. Don't start apologizing for having to have a word about it.

Q. *How do you talk to your housekeeper about missing items?*
A. Again, very straightforward: If you suspect she is stealing, trust your instinct and get rid!

Q. *If you have a housekeeper who comes on a regular basis, must you pay her for the weeks you spend on vacation and don't require her to clean your home?*
A. Yes! Get her to do jobs like kitchen cupboards and the like, things that need doing only occasionally. In any case, if you value her, what about giving her a holiday once in a while?

Q. *How much should you tip your housekeeper over the holidays?*
A. Equivalent of a week's wages.

Q. *Is it necessary to know your housekeeper's last name?*
A. God yes! And get references.

Q. *Is it hard for you not to clean your friend's homes or offer suggestions when you visit them?*
A. I am SO not interested! If any of my pals is apologetic about the state of their place, I reassure them by saying that I am there for their food, drink, and company!

Q. *And lastly, tell us the truth, Aggie—how clean is your house? Do you clean it yourself, or do you have someone come in and clean?*
A. Never as clean as I would like it to be. We have had a cleaner ever since I went back to work after I had my first child. I find

the day-to-day vacuuming, dusting, et cetera, boring, and love the fact that someone else does it. I am much happier sorting out carpet stains, marks on walls, dirty grouting—even cleaning the oven or the windows. Anything that makes a difference and doesn't have to be done every day!

Dumpipedia

▶ Robert De Niro dumped his housekeeper for stealing a $95,000 pair of diamond drop earrings.

▶ Who played the Keaton's inept housekeeper on *Family Ties*?
- **A.** Dana Delany
- **B.** Geena Davis
- **C.** Laura Dern
- **D.** Lisa Kudrow

▶ Madonna was a housekeeper while studying dance in Manhattan.

▶ Did you know there is Housekeeping Olympics? Teams compete in events that range from "blindfolded bed-making" to "slalom," which features teams of two pushing brooms as they steer soaps and other items through an obstacle course of "wet floor" signs.

▶ True or False? Ann B. Davis who played Alice on *The Brady Bunch* was not the original casting choice.

The answer is B. Geena Davis.

The answer is True. The role originally went to Monty Margetts, but the producers changed their minds when they recast Florence Henderson as Carol Brady.

seventeen

THE ROOMMATE

Signs It's Time to Dump Your Roommate

▶ He asks to borrow a clean pair of your underwear.

▶ He eats your food, while you're eating it.

▶ He speaks in limericks.

▶ He calls you from his bedroom while you're in the kitchen and asks whether you wouldn't mind bringing him a piece of chicken—pretty please!

▶ His girlfriend moves in and redecorates your apartment with kittens and unicorns.

203

No Room for You!

After graduating from college, I sublet a two-bedroom apartment in the West Village from a friend who was moving to Boston to live with her boyfriend. In order for it to be more affordable, I decided to look for a roommate. Enter Rachel, a college friend of a childhood friend of mine. Upon meeting Rachel at a local French bistro, she seemed great. She had a good job, check, appeared put together, check, liked to go out but not bring the party home: check, check. I liked how easygoing she seemed, mentioning how much she hated drama. It was all going so well that I invited her back to the apartment to take a look. Rachel took one glance at the place and was in. "Look, I don't want to rush you, but I kind of need to know if I can move in as soon as possible, since I start a new job in the city next week and I have to get out of my sublet in Jersey City before then." But she *was* rushing me—there's nothing I hate more than being put on the spot. At the same time, I knew how hard it was to find a place to live in Manhattan (let alone find someone you like well enough to live with). I sympathized as I looked long and hard into her desperate, steel-blue eyes and said yes. Then I looked to the heavens above and prayed that I had made the right decision.

Rachel moved in the next day. My minimalist way of living was quickly overtaken by her overcrowded shabby chic aesthetic. We celebrated our first night together as roommates by eating falafel at the Middle Eastern restaurant at the end of the block. One of the things I liked about Rachel was her independent spirit. When the belly dancer approached our table, Rachel was up and out of her seat in no time, dancing and performing as though it was second nature to her. She liked to have fun and, unlike me, wasn't lazy. I liked her sense of adventure and was hoping that some of it would rub off on me.

Things didn't run as smoothly as I would have liked those first few days. I quickly discovered that Rachel was not a morning person. So much so that if I passed her in the hallway before she was officially up, she'd flat out ignore me. Speaking was strictly reserved for after coffee, and not a minute before. Rachel had other habits that I wasn't fully comfortable with, such as walking around the house naked. When I asked her nicely to put a robe on, she said, "I don't know how to use them—they just kind of slide off of me." Really? Hmmm. Then there were her moods. I never knew whether I was coming home to the adventurous Rachel or the bitchy Rachel who would stomp around the apartment in a huff. I grew tired of constantly asking, "Are you okay?"

Then came the duck. Rachel loved duck meat. Duck and eggs, duck with rice, duck sandwiches, you name it: there was always plenty of it to be found in the refrigerator and freezer. Before long, I barely had room for my food. But when I came home one day and opened the fridge only to discover that she had removed the shelves in order to make room for an entire glazed Chinese duck, I had enough of this quack.

"It's the age difference," she said.

"What is?" I replied.

"The fact that we don't jive as well as we had hoped." I had to take that one in for a moment, since there were only two years separating us.

"I don't think so," I said. And for the first time since living together, Rachel tied her robe and sat down next to me.

"Look, I've lived a little more than you, had a few more roommates in my time. You're looking for your first job; I've had three. Just try relaxing more, you'll be fine. I promise." But I wasn't asking for that kind of promise. I wanted her to not leave her duck heads lying around scaring me. I wanted her to be less moody and not leave her dental floss everywhere—like between the pillows on the couch, or hanging from the leaves of a plant. I wanted the easy-to-get-along-with girl from the West Village café where we met, the one who hated drama—not created it.

After our talk, I opted to stay out more than usual and hide in my bedroom when I was home. Rachel continued to stomp around the apartment, slamming cabinets and doors and letting me know when she was annoyed. I prayed that she would move out, but I knew that she wouldn't willingly leave such a great apartment. My prayers were finally answered a month later when the woman from whom I had been subletting the apartment called from Boston to tell me that she and her boyfriend had broken up and that she was moving back to New York. She invited me to stay on, but that meant that Rachel would have to take all that life experience of hers and find a new roommate—hopefully one who liked duck.

What I Learned

Over the years I've had so many roommates that I can barely remember half their names. Once I passed a girl on the street and stared right into her eyes with a look that read, "How do I know you?" I kid you not, she looked at me and said, "Roommates. NYU." Snap! The players may have changed over the years, but the one thing that was consistent was me hiding in my room, terrified of speaking to any of them when something was wrong. The one time I did speak up was with Rachel and her all-consuming obsession with duck. The problem was that I let the conversation run away from me. I allowed her to take control of our dialogue—big mistake. I wish we had come up with some house rules before she had moved in. At the very least, I wouldn't have to walk around carrying the image of a whole duck hanging in my refrigerator in my head. Thankfully, I no longer have to live with a roommate. However, if ever the day comes and I need to live with one, I know exactly what to do.

Laying the Groundwork

▶ The key to a successful roommate relationship is having open lines of communication. So sit down with your roommate and make a list of house rules. Whenever possible, try to do it before moving in together. If it's too late, do it now.

▶ Have your roommate sign the agreement. Tell him that if either one of you continues to break the rules, the other person has the right to ask the offender to move out.

▶ Suggest monthly house meetings (or every few months). This is your chance to break down any resentment that tends to spring up, such as when one roommate feels he is buying all the toilet paper or cleaning house more than the other. Check-ins are a way of keeping the peace by clearing the air. Perhaps you want to suggest sitting down together when paying the bills each month. Having a pre-established time to talk helps ensure that everyone has time to think about what he's going to say.

▶ Warn him. If your roommate continues to break the house rules, sit down with him and bring it to his attention. If you're always the one nagging him, ask your roommate if there's a better way to discuss these problems in future. Would he prefer you to leave him a note? Tell your roommate that you both agreed to these rules and had you not, you wouldn't have moved in.

▶ Study your lease, paying special attention to clauses pertaining to roommates. If you don't understand your lease, take a copy of it and pay a visit to your local fair housing council or tenants' union and have them explain it to you.

▶ Learn how to legally terminate your lease with your roommate under your state's current law. For example, California allows you to terminate your lease if your roommate fails to pay rent, violates the lease, damages the property, uses the apartment for illegal activities, or seriously interferes with other tenants. Look for loopholes such as no pets, no smoking, no businesses allowed—anything that you can nail your roommate with.

▶ Find out whether your city or town allows landlords to designate a "master tenant." This is a long-term tenant who was living in the apartment first. Master tenants have the right to choose and evict other tenants even if both names are on the lease. Call your landlord and ask to be made the master tenant.

▶ If your roommate is trashing your apartment, notify your landlord immediately. Even though both of you are responsible for the damage (if both of you are on the lease), many landlords look favorably upon cooperative tenants.

▶ Have another roommate lined up.

▶ Write down all expenses that need to be settled: utility bills, rent, household appliances.

▶ Get back all your personal belongings.

Warning: Don't try and settle grievances over alcohol. It may sound like a good idea, but alcohol tends to loosen tongues and, before you know it, tempers flare.

Basic House Rules

1. Rent: Discuss who pays the landlord. You? Him? Both of you? Set a date each month that you will provide your rent check. Make it clear that there is no wiggle room here; if he doesn't pay rent on time, he will be asked to move out.

2. Utility bills: Who pays and when?

3. Noise levels: Figure out a sound level that both of you can live with.

4. Cleaning: Wash dishes immediately, or in the morning? Come up with a schedule of who cleans what (and when) or discuss splitting the cost of a housekeeper. Do not accept "We'll figure it out" as an answer. Figure it out now.

5. Smoking: In the house or outside?

6. Food: Is everything up for grabs or does each roommate have his own shelf in the fridge?

7. Household appliances and furnishings: Do you split the cost, or does one roommate pay for the furniture and own it outright?

8. Overnight guests: How many are you okay with? Every night, once a month?

9. Moving out: How many days' notice should you give? Experts suggest thirty days.

How to Dump 'Em

Caution: No one likes to be forced from his home. Show empathy, but keep your emotional distance.

STRIKE THREE: YOOUUUUUU'RE OUT!

Hopefully, your name is the only one on the lease, so you can use that to your advantage. However, if both of your names are on the lease, you're in a trickier situation. This is why it's important to have him agree to the house rules.

1. Set a time and place for your house meeting. Give your roommate plenty of time to make it.

2. Start with something positive or pay him a compliment. *"We've known each other for ten years, and I value our friendship."*

3. Remind him of your roommate agreement and the times you've warned him. *"But as you know, I've tried many times to ask you to abide by the rules of the house that you and I both agreed to before moving in."*

4. Ask him to move out, plain and simple. *"This is a tough conversation to have, but I'm going to have to ask you to move out. Take the month and find another place to live. I appreciate your understanding."*

   Warning: If he asks for a second chance or an extension, be careful before agreeing, because chances are that he will want an additional one down the road.

5. Let him react. Be prepared for him to be angry or upset. Your job is to listen but not react in a way that will encourage an argument. Allow your roommate to have his feelings heard, but make sure you don't get sucked in by them. Be firm with your decision.

6. Discuss final rent and utilities and how you'd like to make the transition to the new roommate. If you already have a new roommate lined up, let him know the date when this person is moving in.

7. Thank him again for understanding, and, if appropriate, offer to help him find a place.

WRITE A LETTER

While it's encouraged to talk to your roommate in person, it isn't always an option. I once had a friend who knew that his room-mate wanted him to move out, so every time his roommate tried to have a sit down or schedule a meeting, he made sure to be busy or unavailable. It got my friend another six months. Finally his roommate had enough and wrote him a letter telling him he had thirty days to move out.

If your roommate is avoiding you and continues to not show up when you ask him to, write him a letter; go over everything, his deadline for moving out, the final rent payment, any money owed, outstanding utility bills, and so forth. In situations where you both split the cost of a household item such as a toaster, consider giving it to him. It's worth it, if only for your own peace of mind.

GIVE ME BACK MY ROOM . . . MATE

For those whose name is the only one on the lease, apologize to your roommate and then let him know that you'd like his room back. Give him plenty of time to find a new living situation and a reason, such as you're converting the room into an office or that you're asking your boy/girlfriend to move in with you. Don't have a relationship? Get one.

MOVIN' ON UP!

Sometimes the best and easiest thing to do is move out. Weigh your options carefully, because no matter how good a deal you have with your current rent or how much you love your current digs, is it really worth it to continue living with a roommate you don't like?

In a Pinch

"UH OH, GUESS WHO HAS MONO!"

You know what sucks? Coming down with mono. Who doesn't love having a sore throat, fever, muscle soreness, and fatigue for a couple of months? I don't, and neither will your roommate. For those of you really in a pinch, tell your roommate that you've come down with a bad case of mononucleosis and your doctor said that rest and relaxation is the only way to get better—so you'll be camping out at home for the next couple of months. Cough whenever he walks into a room, neglecting to cover your mouth. Try keeping the windows sealed shut so your place stays nice and stuffy. If your roommate opens a window, shout "Brrrrrrr!" and shake a little. Apologize, mentioning that you'd totally understand if he wanted to move out (cough, cough)! Hey, you'd move out if the tables were turned, especially since mono is highly contagious and takes forever to get over. If he suggests that perhaps you'd be more comfortable going home to recover, remind him that this is your home.

TELL YOUR ROOMMATE THAT YOU FOUND RELIGION AND ARE PRAYING FOR HIM. HALLELUJAH!

Stop by your local religious center and pick up as many pamphlets as possible without getting arrested. Then strategically litter your apartment with them. The bathroom, your roommate's sock drawer, his book bag or briefcase—these are all good spots. Carry your Bible around the house, reciting passages and asking whether he would be willing to pray with you. Try making a flyer for biweekly prayer meetings at your apartment, and then ask your roommate to proofread it. Whenever possible, slip a religious quote or passage into conversations. For example, if your roommate says, "Can you pass me an apple?" respond with, "If you like apples, I have a wonderful story to tell you about apples and creation." It shouldn't take long before your roommate looks for another apartment.

INTRODUCE YOUR ROOMMATE TO YOUR NEW FRIEND, STRAIGHT FROM THE SLAMMER

Go through your address book and carefully choose a friend who looks like he could have gone to prison—then ask him to do you a little favor. Dress him in denim and have him stop by for drinks on a night you know your roommate will be home. Ask him to put on his best "I mean business" face and walk through your apartment asking how much things cost. Then have him say a few of the following things to your roommate:

"So, where are you from exactly?"

"What's your date of birth again?"

"You ever gone out with anyone who's been in the slammer before? Would you like to?"

"Uh oh, I think I might be having another one of my episodes again. I feel it coming on."

Have him show up whenever possible. If your roommate hasn't moved out by now, pick a day when you're sure you can get home before your roommate and then mess the apartment up, including his bedroom. When your roommate comes home, pretend that you are in the middle of cleaning it up. When he asks what happened, be casual and say, "Nothing really, I was just cleaning up a bit. But, hey, let me ask you a question, you didn't happen to give my buddy a key to our apartment, did you?" When he asks why, say, "Nothing, I'm sure it's nothing. Never mind." Then go to your bedroom.

What to Do if Your Roommate Refuses to Move Out

1. Review the relevant tenant laws. The legalities surrounding eviction of a roommate vary greatly from state to state.

2. Consult a fair housing representative in your area and explain your situation.

3. Housing mediation: Mediators are neutral third parties who (for a fraction of the cost of a lawyer) can help roommates settle their problems without having to go to court. Look for one in your local Yellow Pages.

4. Call a landlord-tenant attorney and have him represent you.

Susie Stein

**OWNER OF ROOMMATE FINDERS, IN BUSINESS SINCE 1977.
THEY'VE SUCCESSFULLY HELPED OVER 250,000 PEOPLE FIND
COMPATIBLE ROOMMATES.**

www.RoommateFinders.net

Q. *What's the biggest mistake people make when choosing a roommate?*

A. Trying to find an exact clone of themselves.

Q. *What's the best way to handle roommate disputes?*

A. Not let them happen in the first place. Everyone needs to communicate from the beginning exactly what is important to them and then try to give the other person some slack—as long as it's within reason.

Q. *What are the signs that it's time to dump your roommate?*

A. The first sign that it's time to dump them is when they start acting disrespectfully toward you, your friends, or the property.

Q. *Is it better to have one person sign a lease, or should all roommates sign it?*

A. Everyone needs to have some sort of written agreement that is binding, whether it is a lease or just a simple piece of paper that outlines what each person's responsibilities are going to be.

Q. *How do you know if your roommate is about to dump you?*

A. They change the locks.

Q. *How do you dump a roommate?*

A. Basically, if the transaction is initially handled as a business contract, there should not be any problems dumping a roommate. If the parties have agreed in writing from the beginning what is important to them—and it is signed and agreed to by each of them—all they need to do is remind each other of the agreement. For example—if you I don't like dishes in the sink and agreed to either wash them or put them in the dishwasher as soon as you're done. Oops! You have a huge assignment at work and don't have time to put them away. No problem, understandable. But if you leave the dishes in the sink every single day and they begin to accumulate and create a mess, that is obviously a problem. If you can't communicate, then agree to both go your separate ways.

Being fair, reasonable, and communicating before problems get out of hand keeps most things on an even keel. If you think you are being dumped, you need to make sure you are treated fairly. Refer to the business contract you signed and agreed to and don't be so stubborn that you can't say, "I'm sorry, and I will try to do better."

Q. *What do you do if your roommate refuses to leave?*

A. You change the locks.

Q. *What's the best way to deal with who gets what when roommates move out? (Meaning furniture, appliances, and so on.)*

A. Keep the receipts and pay or make an even exchange.

Q. *What's the one piece of advice you can offer potential new roommates who are reading this?*

A. Live and let live.

Q. What's the craziest roommate story you've heard?

A. I heard a story about two girls who moved in together and one was a size 8 and the other was a size 14. The size 14 was borrowing the size 8's clothes. Is that even possible?

▶ Suzanne Somers was dumped by the producers of *Three's Company* due to various disputes and a very public lawsuit.

▶ Tommy Lee Jones and former vice president Al Gore were roommates at Harvard. Rumor has it the two of them served as inspiration for the character of Oliver in *Love Story* (written by fellow Harvard alum Erich Segal).

▶ *Roommates* was a 1995 movie starring Peter Falk and D. B. Sweeney about a boy who, after losing both his parents at a young age, is raised by his stubborn grandfather.

▶ Owen Wilson and Wes Anderson were roommates at the University of Texas.

▶ Robin Williams was a roommate at Juilliard to which famous actor?
   A. John Malkovich
   B. Christopher Reeve
   C. John Lithgow
   D. Billy Crystal

The answer is B. Christopher Reeve.

part five
DOCTORS, LAWYERS, INDIAN CHIEFS

eighteen

THE CONTRACTOR

Signs It's Time to Dump Your Contractor

▶ He uses your favorite Italian hand towels to mop up paint spills.

▶ He knocks down the wrong wall.

▶ You ask to see his license and he laughs.

▶ He tells you he's tired and asks about sleeping over.

▶ You notice that every time he leaves, your toothbrush is wet.

Putting Out a Contract
on Your Contractor

A few years ago, my sister Susan was in need of a contractor to expand her kitchen in order to accommodate her ever-growing family. Her friend Mabel said she had "the perfect man" for the job: her daughter's much older boyfriend. He had just built a deck for Mabel and she was beyond happy. What better way to hire a contractor than to have a firsthand recommendation from someone Susan trusted?

But the "perfect man" showed up at my sister's house with a less than perfect attitude. Believing that all people possess a goodness within, Susan was more than willing to look past it. Bob was a crotchety old bastard, despite the fact that he couldn't have been more than forty years old. Etiquette was not his strength—something he had no problem sharing with Susan. "I belch a lot. It's the way I was made." And then he gave my sister just a little taste of what was to come.

Bob the Builder (as my nephew liked to call him) took a tour of the house, bringing with him some impressive tools. He banged on a few walls, took out his measuring tape, scribbled some notes, and then presented Susan and her husband, Yosef, with his game plan. He would take down one wall, open up another (giving them a view of the family room from the kitchen), and remove a bathroom. Susan and Yosef, who had no building experience whatsoever, accepted his plan as well as his payment schedule, which required paying half up front. No contract was ever presented or signed.

My sister had just one requirement—that they always have a working kitchen, because feeding a family of six was not cheap. "Done," said Bob the Builder, and with no receipt and little more than a handshake, the deal was done. He said he'd start the following day, but his "following day" must have been some kind of contractor code for two and a half weeks later. When Susan called Bob to see where he was, her calls went straight to voicemail. Then one morning as the kids were being strapped into the family van, getting ready to head to school, Bob the Builder appeared with his crew. Susan reluctantly let him into the house, less than thrilled that the construction would be unsupervised until she returned.

Three weeks later, walls had come down, with dirt and what was later identified as lead contaminating the kitchen, family room, and children's toys. The kitchen had been turned into a war zone, with dangerous equipment strewn everywhere. As far as the working kitchen went—well, there wasn't one. When Susan approached Bob to let him know of her disapproval, she was met with a giant manwich-style belch, followed by a demand for more money. "My guys won't show up tomorrow if you don't pay 'em more money. Up to you. (Buuuuuuuuuurp!)"

To add insult to injury, Bob told Susan that the main wall he had demolished had a chimney hiding behind it. He told Susan to find a way to work around it. Dumbfounded, Susan asked him how he had failed to notice that before he started the job. Did the furnace in the basement not tip him off? Bob's response? "Shit happens"; words you don't want to hear from your contractor.

Susan and Yosef spent a sleepless night, wondering how they had managed to get themselves into such a giant mess. It was time to cut their losses and let Bob go. Susan prepared a speech telling him where he could put those rusty old tools of his—and secretly wishing that she could actually show him. As Susan and Yosef watched the sun rise, Susan paced back and forth, rehearsing her speech. When Bob's car pulled up in the driveway, she headed downstairs.

Bob was right; the crew didn't show up. Susan walked up alongside Bob, who was now drinking a Tab and peacefully staring into the woods outside of her house. Instead of launching into her prepared speech, she looked out the window into the woods and said, "You know, Bob, I think we're all set. We've got it from here. Thanks anyway." And, with one last giant belch, Bob the Builder was history.

What I Learned

I'm a lot like Susan, so I most likely would have done the exact same thing and hired the first person recommended to me without doing any research or asking him if he had a valid contractor license by the state. I was outraged to discover just how easy it is for anyone to call himself a contractor. Print out a card from your computer and voila, guess who's a licensed contractor? You are!

So here's what I learned. Never pay more than 10 percent up front. If your contractor says he needs the money to buy materials, be skeptical, because most reputable contractors have accounts set up at the shops they do business with. The only power you have over your contractor is money, so come up with a schedule of payment that reflects work done on the house. And make sure that you get everything in writing, from a complete list of materials to a detailed summary of work to be done, a total price of everything, and some kind of clause stating penalties if the job doesn't come in on time. Before signing the contract, make sure you insist on a three-day grace period. This allows you to change your mind as well as come up with the questions you may have forgotten to ask. Many states require the three days by law. Spend that time going over every line in your contract, including the fine print; don't just stuff it in a drawer.

Also make sure that your contractor and his workers are insured. Don't assume they are or you may find yourself in some serious legal drama. Workman's compensation insurance protects you in case a worker is injured on your property and general liability insurance covers you in case a contractor damages your property. Get a copy of both insurance cards and confirm they are valid.

Next, go over all the ground rules with your contractor before he starts the job. Hand him a list of guidelines for him and his crew to follow. It's up to you to list which rooms in your house are off limits as well as suggest proper etiquette, especially around children. Agree to work hours that you're comfortable with and point out proper storage places. You'd be surprised how many workers think that your entire driveway is grounds for their tools and materials. The same goes for bathrooms: Do you want them using a specific bathroom in your house or would you prefer to rent an outhouse?

By taking the time to learn as much as possible about the work you want to have done in your house and the materials needed, you become savvier and less likely to be tricked. Web sites like AngiesList.com and Contractors.com can be extremely helpful. They've even done most of the legwork for you, researching and reviewing licensed contractors as well as providing sample contracts. In addition, Contractors.com has an easy-to-understand glossary of terms seen in most contracts and a cost estimator that calculates your project costs.

Contractor Scams

1. Be on the lookout for criminals who pose as door-to-door home repair contractors. They rip off homeowners and often prey on the elderly; they attract their targets by offering complimentary inspections and then offer to fix the (often fictional) problem immediately for cash. Most use toll-free (800) telephone numbers and drive vehicles with out-of-state license plates or arrive in an unmarked truck or van.

2. They say they have leftover materials from another job and can offer them to you for a greatly discounted price.

3. They use "sealant" that's nothing more than watered-down brand-name product.

4. They exaggerate the number of paint cans used.

5. They charge homeowners for a new roof, but in fact they just slide a few pieces of newer material on top of the existing roof.

Laying the Groundwork

▶ Review your contract and look carefully for an exit clause, which states clearly how problems should be resolved.

▶ Make sure your contractor has a valid contractor's license issued by the state in which you live and not just a business license. A business license only means that he has opened a business; it doesn't prove that he has been trained or licensed as a contractor. Copy the license number, then call your state's licensed contractors' board and verify it along with the company name and number. If the license is from out of state, the law might not protect you. The good news, however, is that you might not be in a legally binding contract. For example, in California it's illegal for anyone to perform construction work on a job totaling $500 or more without the appropriate California license.

▶ Call the Better Business Bureau and see whether your contractor has any violations reported against him.

▶ Warn him. Don't assume your contractor will figure it out himself. You must be an active participant. Don't give him the control. From scheduling to spiraling costs, let him know that you're not happy and allow him to fix things. Poor communication is what leads to spiraling costs. Tell your contractor that he needs to fix the things that are not working.

▶ Send him a certified letter in the mail, writing your concerns in as much detail as possible. You might need this letter as evidence in court, so make a copy for your records.

How to Dump 'Em

Warning: Don't piss off your contractor, as this can lead to serious trouble. Think heavy machinery and open electrical work. The last thing you want to do is give him a reason to cause more damage to your house. So stay calm and collected.

TEARING DOWN THE WALLS

If you've voiced your concerns and still feel like you're not being heard, it's time to sit him down and tell him exactly what you want to have happen.

Warning: If you have a contract with your contractor, you must pay him for the money due, as contracts hold you legally responsible.

STEPS

1. **Arrange for a time to talk.**

2. **Start with a compliment or something positive. For example, *"The new bathtub looks great."***

3. **Dump him. *"But I've asked you to fix the sink and given you many opportunities to do so. At this point, I've run out***

of time, patience, and now money. I'd like to pay you for the work you've done and call it quits."

4. **Allow him to respond. He may try to work it out with you.**

5. **If he agrees to be paid and leave, have him sign lien waivers preventing him from legally going after your property to recover money.** *"I appreciate your understanding. If you would just sign this waiver, I'd be happy to write you a check."*

6. **Thank him and pay him for the work he has completed— once he's signed the waiver.**

WWW.ANGIESLIST.COM

Don't want to dump your contractor? Have Angie do it for you! AngiesList.com is a Web site that allows homeowners to share real-life experiences with local service companies. It also provides a third-party service to help members restore dialogue with their contractors. For those who qualify, Angie's List will contact a contractor on your behalf and potentially print the results in its magazine. If your contractor doesn't respond to the complaints, he just might have his name printed in the magazine's "Penalty Box."

ARBITRATOR/MEDIATOR

Personality differences and money issues are the major reasons why things don't work out with contractors. In these cases, one of the best options is sitting down with a neutral third party mediator. He can help you resolve your differences at very little cost and can be found in the Yellow Pages, through your local Department of Consumer Affairs, or the American Arbitration Association at www.adr.org. Mediation is less formal than going to court, costs less, and is nowhere near as stressful. The other advantage is that mediation and arbitration does not go on public record, giving your contractor more incentive to work things out. Mediators found on the American Arbitration Association Web site have a minimum of fifteen years of professional experience. Arbitrators can also be found on their site. They are lawyers or judges trained in dispute management whose decisions are final and binding.

COURT

When all else fails, take your contractor to court. Depending on the amount involved (and the state you live in), you may be able to go to small claims court, but be aware that there's not much a court can do to guarantee that you get paid. In addition, it can take a long time to get a court date. One person I spoke to had to wait over nine months. If you pursue going to court, be sure to provide solid evidence that your contractor is responsible for your problem—and most important, make sure your contractor has the money to pay you if he loses.

In a Pinch

HOME MAKEOVER

Guess who got chosen to be on a home makeover show? You did! Let your contractor know that from this point on you no longer need his services, as yours will be the featured home on an upcoming episode of the show. How lucky are you?!

Q&A
Adam Carolla
ACTOR, COMEDIAN, AND RADIO HOST

Q. *What's the best way to dump a contractor?*
A. You've grown apart and you want to start seeing other contractors. Or you can use the one I use: "It's not you, it's me."

Q. *What are the red flags that your contractor sucks and you need to dump him?*
A. Here are the warning signs that he is a bad builder: if you find out he knows how to work a computer for anything other than giving invoices; or he wants to head anywhere on the weekend other than the river; or he's not a racist/bigot then you have got a bad builder on your hands.

Q. *How do you know for sure your contractor isn't robbing you blind?*
A. Robbing is the least of your worries; it's the raping that's gonna hurt.

Q. *What's the one thing most homeowners forget to ask their contractors before signing the contract?*
A. Their astrological sign.

Q. *Is there a way to put a clause in a contract to allow someone to break up with his contractor should he need to?*
A. Yeah, it's done all the time—it's called a pre-nup'.

Q. *How do you get your contractor to actually show up on time?*
A. Make sure you always owe him money.

Q. *How do you get a contractor to complete the job on time?*
A. Refer to the above answer.

Q. *Can you ask your contractor to wear deodorant?*
A. You could, but then you'd have to deal with all of the subcontractors, laborers, etc. Better you just put a dollop of menthylatum rub on your upper lip, like the autopsy scene from *Silence of the Lambs.*

Q. *How do you tell your contractor to keep his mitts out of your refrigerator?*
A. Tell him you are vegan.

Q. *What's the one tip every homeowner should know?*
A. How to hide porn.

Q. *Is it true you actually have an asteroid named after you?*
A. Yes, and later this year, when it collides with Texas, I will have a lot of explaining to do.

DUMPIPEDIA

▸ According to Harvard's Joint Center for Housing Studies, Americans spend $155 billion each year remodeling their homes.

▸ Looking for a contract for you and your potential contractor to sign? Check out the American Institute of Architects' Web site at www.aia.org and download one.

▸ Remodeling an attic bedroom is the best investment for an American homeowner, according to *Remodeling* magazine's 2007 Cost vs. Value Report.

▸ Contractors charge lower rates (by as much as 5–7 percent) for work during their slow time.

▸ Workers are more productive and efficient in cooler weather than in the heat of summer.

nineteen

THE ACCOUNTANT

Signs It's Time to Dump Your Accountant

▶ She counts on her fingers.

▶ She asks *you* what a 1099 is.

▶ She complains to you about how difficult it is to be dyslexic.

▶ She tells you that it's okay to create imaginary dependents—like the family of squirrels that live outside your bedroom window.

▶ She tells you this is the last time she'll be able to do your taxes for the next five years: two years with good behavior.

Take Your Money and Run

I'm a fairly lazy person. If I don't *have* to do something, I probably won't. Exercise? No thanks. Eat healthier? Only if it tastes good. Do my own taxes? Not a chance. My idea of doing taxes is placing a bunch of receipts in a shopping bag and, come March, sending them off by certified mail to my accountant Joe in New Hampshire, a state that I haven't lived in for years.

Accountants just weren't something I thought about—until last year. While attending a dinner party, I found myself in the middle of a conversation that revolved around accountants. It was a "my accountant is better than your accountant" discussion. However, because everyone at the table worked in the entertainment business, the conversation sounded a lot like a pitch for a television game show. "Two people, the same job, and two crazzzzzzy accountants battle it out! Who will save the most money come tax day?! Find out tonight—live!" As I sat there listening to the number of write-offs these people were getting each year, I was blown away. All of them were writers and entertainers like me; the only difference was that they were seeing hotshot Hollywood accountants. It was time for me to see a fancy Hollywood accountant.

The first step would be breaking the news to my father, who I knew would defend Joe, since he had done our family's taxes for forty years. I was prepared for that conversation. What I wasn't ready for was my dad telling me that Joe hadn't done my taxes in years; someone named Cassie was doing them. Huh? Cassie? Who's Cassie? For over a decade I had been sending my taxes with personalized notes wishing Joe and his family well, and all that time they'd actually been handed over to someone named Cassie? According to my dad, Joe still worked at the firm, but had moved up in rank and was only handling "big" clients now.

I was pissed off, yet curious at the same time. Who was this Cassie? How old was she? Had she always wanted to be an accountant? Did she like her job? Apparently both my dad and my sister knew her quite well. I picked up the phone and called my sister to ask her about Cassie. "That's so funny," she said. "I'm IMing with her right now!" What? Was everyone friends with her? I felt deceived. I couldn't comprehend how it had never occurred to her to call me and introduce herself. I imagined her reading all my notes to Joe, giggling, and then tossing them in the trash.

The next moment, in a rare fit of anger, I picked up the phone and dialed the accounting firm. I was going to dump Cassie. I'd ask to speak to her, introduce myself, and then dump away. One ring, two rings, three rings, and then the pick-up, "This is Joe." Joe? I completely froze and hung up. For the next seven seconds I sat there wondering why a receptionist hadn't answered the phone. Then I realized it was because I called Joe on his cell phone, not the office. The next moment, my phone rang. I glanced at the caller ID and saw it was Joe calling, so I did the only thing I could do in that moment; I picked up the phone, and in my best Chinese accent answered, "Lucky Chang's Restaurant."

When I heard Joe say, "Jodyne?" I repeated, "Lucky Chang's, how may I help you?"

There was an awkward pause. Then he said, "I'm confused. I'm looking for Jodyne." Another pause. I knew in every bone in my body that I should just drop the accent and confess instead of keeping this horrible charade going.

Instead, I said, "Wrong numbah!" And with that, I hung up the phone and ended my relationship with Joe and Cassie.

What I Learned

According to *Consumer Reports*, fewer than half of all U.S. taxpayers fill out their own tax forms—which means that more than 50 percent of all Americans are handing over their financial records to other people. I wonder how many of them are actually taking the time to go over each page of their tax returns before signing. I hate to admit it, but I never do. As soon as I get the envelope from my accountant's office, I scribble my John Hancock and off it goes. But whether you have a CPA, an EA, or a tax attorney filing for you, the bottom line is that you're the one responsible for the information on your tax return. This chapter taught me how important it is to take the time to go over each page of your return before sending the envelope off to Uncle Sam or be prepared to suffer the consequences.

One of the biggest complaints from accountants I spoke with was that their clients were not providing them with enough information. One CPA had a client get married, change jobs, and have a baby all within the past year and not tell him. He eventually figured it out, but it took a lot of time and energy. It's not wise to leave it up to one's accountant to connect the financial dots. This means reporting any changes you've made over the year that might affect your taxes such as marriages, real estate ventures, children, or a new job.

It took talking to one person who got audited to scare me into being more involved with my taxes. While the old me never asked my accountant any questions, the new me has come up with a whole list of them while researching this chapter. Guess who's not so lazy anymore?

Laying the Groundwork

▶ Make sure that you have a copy of your last tax return. If you don't, call your accountant's office and request one.

▶ Decide how much you wish to share with your accountant about your reasons for leaving. If she's made errors on your return, think about bringing them to her attention. It's useful feedback.

▶ Have a new accountant lined up. If you need help, check out www.GoodAccountants.com or www.Accountantratingz.com. Both are excellent sites that rate accountants and tax preparers in your area.

How to Dump 'Em

I DEDUCT YOU!

According to the U.S. General Accounting Office, taxpayers overpay their taxes by an estimated $1 billion each year. This means a lot more of you should be dumping your accountants—and fast.

For those of you with very little contact with your accountant other than handing her an envelope each year, call her office and tell her your decision. Have the office take you off her mailing list and ask for a copy of your last year's return if you don't already have it. If, however, your relationship with your accountant is more personal, call or at the very least write her a nice letter or e-mail. After all, she may have spent time discussing your financial future and just may have a vested interest in your success. She deserves the heads-up.

1. **Call, e-mail, or write her.**

2. **Start with a compliment or something positive.** *"Thank you for taking care of my taxes these past _____ years."*

3. **Dump her. Keep it short and sweet.** If you want to give her feedback, do so; otherwise, try, *"After giving it much thought, I've decided that it's time for me to change accountants. Thank you for everything."*

4. **Allow her to respond.** If she asks you for a second chance, be firm. *"I'm sorry, my decision has been made."*

5. **Thank her for understanding and say good-bye.**

NO LONGER FEASIBLE

CPA, EA, or tax attorney—do you know the difference? All CPAs are accountants, but not all accountants are CPAs. Certified public accountants must have at least a bachelor's degree in accounting and business administration and have passed a state-licensing exam. They offer investment services, mortgage advice, and estate planning, and set up retirement plans. An enrolled agent, on the other hand, is a federally licensed tax specialist who doesn't necessarily have any formal education. EAs must pass a national qualifying exam and take twenty-four hours of continuing education per year in order to renew their license. EAs are able to handle a wide variety of returns and tend to cost much less than a CPA or a tax attorney (the most expensive of all tax professionals since they had to pass a state bar exam specializing in tax law). Whatever accountant you're seeing, another way to dump her is by letting her know that you've decided to go in a new direction with your taxes and are going to start seeing a different kind of tax specialist.

WHAT YOU SAY: *"Because my taxes are pretty straightforward this year, I've decided to save money by going with an enrolled agent instead of a CPA. If my finances become more complex in the future, I'll be in touch. Thanks for everything."*

BE PREPARED FOR HER TO SAY: *"Nobody's taxes are easy. You get what you pay for."*

FINAL WORD: *"You might be right, but for the time being I'm willing to take my chances."*

NEW KID ON THE BLOCK

Looking for an easy way to dump your accountant? Tell her you've decided to start doing your own taxes. The IRS makes it easy with its Web site at www.irs.gov, where you can download all the forms you need (as well as the necessary instructions). It even has a hotline for taxpayers, 1-800-TAX-1040, which the IRS reports has a 91 percent accuracy rate.

In a Pinch

GOING TO THE CHAPEL

Tell your accountant that you just got married, and from now on you'll be filing joint returns with your partner. Explain how attached your significant other is to her accountant and thank her for all her help.

MOVIN' ON UP!

Guess who's moving out of state? You are. If your accountant tells you that she can do your taxes in any state, let her know how important it is to you to have quality face-to-face time.

Bruce Miller

ENROLLED AGENT FOR OVER TWENTY-ONE YEARS
SPECIALIZING IN FILM, TELEVISION, AND MUSIC.

Partner at Bruce Miller & Associates in Sherman Oaks, California.

Q. *Why use an accountant?*
A. Tax law is complex and getting more so each year. The IRS spends a significant portion of their time and resources correcting errors on self-prepared returns. TurboTax and online software are not substitutes for trained professionals.

Q. *Why do people dread going to their accountants?*
A. If I had a dollar for every time I've heard, "I would rather go to the dentist," I'd be two years closer to retirement. Everyone's money is hard to come by, and we are the bearers of the bad news of how much of it is going to be taken away.

Q. *What should someone do if she discovers that her accountant has made a mistake on her taxes? Who's responsible?*
A. They should notify the firm or the individual right away and get an explanation of how it happened. After it has been explained, ask how they are going to fix or address it—and will they be paying all interest and penalties?

Q. *What's the best way to dump your accountant?*
A. In person, if you have the nerve, but telephone, letter, or e-mail will also work. Let them know why you're leaving. If the fees are too high, too many unnecessary errors, bad attitude, or a difference of opinion on how aggressive the deductions should be, etc.,

let them know. If you leave with no comment, they can never possibly fix the problem.

Q. *What's the biggest mistake people make with their taxes?*
A. They routinely think that every dollar of deductible expense equals one dollar of reduced taxes. I paid $25,000 in mortgage interest and gave $1,000 to charity, so my taxes should go down by $26,000, is what I usually hear.

Q. *What's the most exaggerated deduction people tend to claim?*
A. Charitable deductions for silent auction items purchased when they are not entitled to them and overstated value of goods donated is a big one. For business deductions, the percentage of business use of auto, meals, and gifts are also up there.

Q. *What's the strangest deduction one of your clients tried to claim?*
A. Probably the office security system that consisted of dog food and vet bills.

Q. *What's your favorite accounting joke?*
A. What do accountants use for birth control? Their personalities!

Q. *Who's the better accountant, Norm from* Cheers *or Henry from* Ugly Betty?
A. Norm. He's the "everyman."

DUMPIPEDIA

▶ The U.S. government dumped the onetime "Big Five" accounting firm Arthur Andersen after the firm was found guilty of criminal charges in connection to its handling of the auditing of energy company Enron.

▶ The IRS processed approximately 135 million individual income tax returns in 2007.

▶ In 2005, 1.2 million returns were audited by the IRS.

▶ Comedian Bob Newhart started out as an accountant; so did jazz musician Kenny G.

▶ Ohio State University is home to the Accounting Hall of Fame, which honors outstanding contributions to the profession.

▶ The first CPA exam was given in New York in what year?
   A. 1786
   B. 1896
   C. 1928

The answer is B. 1896.

twenty

THE LAWYER

Signs It's Time to Dump Your Lawyer

▶ Her law degree comes from the back of a matchbook.

▶ Her idea of a case is Bud Lite.

▶ She applauds anytime counsel makes a particularly salient point.

▶ Her billable hours include trips to Hawaii.

▶ The opposing counsel high-five each other when they see your attorney enter the courtroom.

Holding Her in Contempt

When the great flood happened in my apartment garage (due to my landlord's negligence [see chapter 8]), the six of us whose cars were totaled banded together in search of a lawyer. It was time to hold our landlord responsible for his actions.

The alpha male of our group of six stepped up and made an appointment for us to see a highfalutin' Beverly Hills lawyer. I showed up, dropped off my rented car with the law firm's complimentary valet service, and greeted my neighbors in the lobby, all of whom were dressed up and ready for battle. We entered the waiting room, which felt more like a VIP lounge at a nightclub than it did a law firm, with mood lighting, an espresso bar with a barista, and platters of panini. We sat, drank our fancy coffee, and vented about our lack of heat, our leaky faucets, and our constantly running toilets. As the caffeine made its way into our bloodstreams, we got increasingly riled up. We were mad as hell at our landlord, and we were not going to take it anymore. Walter, our slumlord, was going down!

Sean, our big-time 90210 attorney, had all the energy and excitement you could hope for in a lawyer. We sat in his high-rise office complete with city views and listened to him talk. The only problem was that I couldn't make out a single word of what he was saying. In addition to all the legalese he was speaking, he had a very strong accent. French? It had some kind of twang to it, so I was thrown. As he continued to talk, my eyes wandered to his wall, where I noticed various posters of hockey players and maple leaves. Hmm. That's not very French. When I spotted his law school diploma, I squinted at it and the mystery was solved: Université de Montréal. *Canadien*! I still had no idea what was coming out of his mouth, but watching him talk, I was captivated; his natural charisma charmed the pants off me. What

And what I did hear, I liked, such as "It iz tyme to tayk yur land-lord down!" That was followed with a giant Celine Dion fist punch to the chest. "No' who iz with me?!" We cheered him as he confidently ran around the room, slapping our hands like a baseball player who hit a home run and is rounding home plate. When the cheers died down, the alpha male of our group brought up the dreaded money issue. How much was all of this going to cost? "You geeve me petite retainer and the rest you leeve do me. Get me ze leezes of all of you, I file, and we discuz the rezt. No worry. Weez going to roll in za dough." So we paid him une pe-tite retainer and left his office beaming with excitement. We had a lawyer—a Beverly Hills one, to boot. This was actually going to happen. The ball was rolling, and it felt empowering.

A few days later, after he received our paperwork, Sean called me. It's funny that the one person who understood his accent the least was the one he chose to call. I assumed it was because I worked from home, so I was easier to reach, but I later found out I was the only one who gave him her real number. He was even harder to understand on the phone than in person.

I kept repeating, "I'm sorry?! Come again?"

This only made him shout. I managed to make out the follow-ing: "More money! A lot more!" Followed by "Nothing filed!"

I waited for a pause, signaling that he was done, and then I said, "Okay, let me talk to my neighbors and see where every-body's at. *Merci*."

The general consensus was everyone wanted Walter to pay, but not if it meant shelling out large amounts of dough. I asked alpha male to dump Sean since he was the one who had found him in the first place, but alpha male suddenly morphed into alpha wuss, staring at the floor and mumbling something about being busy. No one offered to call Sean and tell him the news.

Since lawyers intimidate me, especially ones whom I can't understand, I didn't volunteer to call him. That didn't stop him from calling me, however. I turned off the ringers, hoping he'd go away. When I realized he wouldn't, I took the easiest way out I knew. Knowing that big-time lawyers don't answer the phone themselves, I called his assistant, hoping she'd dump him for me. I told her that we didn't have the money to continue and so we would no longer be going forward with the case. Then I thanked her and asked her to please thank Sean for all of us. I hung up with a giant sigh of relief. I did it. Phew. Five minutes later the phone rang. I looked at the caller ID and saw that it was Sean; naturally, I let it go to voicemail. I did the same thing with the next call after that, and the next, and the next. Until finally, he stopped calling.

What I Learned

I should have fired Sean on the phone instead of calling his assistant and having her do my dirty work. So what if lawyers intimidate me? The only way they're going to stop scaring me is if I put an end to it. This means not allowing them to bulldoze over me. I've seen a number of lawyers over the years, and for the most part I sat back and let them do their jobs—praying they'd come back with good news. I very rarely asked a question, and if I did, I usually didn't understand the answer. On top of that, I've signed countless contracts and other legal documents over the years without so much as glancing at them. If someone said, "sign here," I did, no questions asked. I'm lucky that I've made it this far without getting into some kind of trouble (touch wood). This morning, I turned on the local news and saw hundreds of people lined up in front of their bank, demanding their money. The bank had hit hard times and was forced to close immediately. A lot of those people had signed contracts with the bank without reading the fine print, which stated that their accounts were only insured up to $100,000. If they had more money than the insured amount, they were not protected. That was it for me. From this day forward, I'm not going to sign another document without reading it all first. If I have questions, I'll ask. The same goes for lawyers; if they start speaking legalese or French and I don't understand, I'm putting my hand up and not putting it down until I get an answer that makes sense to me. While researching this chapter, I discovered a slew of Web sites that break down the most common terms that lawyers use and describe what they mean in a way that I can clearly understand. In other words, my days of being intimidated by a lawyer are over.

Laying the Groundwork

▶ If this is not your first time changing attorneys, ask yourself whether it's worth tarnishing your reputation. Courts don't look kindly on those who switch lawyers, and the last thing you want is for them to see you as a problem—think Heather Mills.

▶ Ask your lawyer to discuss a time frame with you for your case. Then be sure to hold her to it (allowing for normal holdups).

▶ Study any written agreements or contracts signed between you and your lawyer. Many of them have clauses that discuss the proper steps to take if you wish to terminate. Consult another lawyer if necessary.

▶ Write down the issues you're having with your lawyer.

▶ Call her and voice all your concerns. Don't be afraid to ask for explanations when necessary. Remember, she works for you, not the other way around.

- Make sure that you actually can dump your lawyer. Some states require the permission of the court, especially with cases close to trial.

- Before dumping your current attorney, have another one lined up to avoid delays. Seek out a personal referral, preferably from someone who has had experience with the same kind of problem. If you can't find one, check out Nolo's lawyer directory at http://lawyers.nolo.com, the American Bar Association at www.abanet.org, or www.Martindale.com. Legal Match (www.legalmatch.com) allows you the opportunity to post your case online for free and then prescreened local attorneys contact you.

- Prepare what you're going to say before dumping your lawyer.

Issues to Address in Final Talk/ Letter to Your Lawyer

1. Getting back your file: Set a deadline and let her know how you want to receive it. Will you pick it up, or should she send it somewhere? Be aware that in some states you can't get back your file until all costs have been paid in full.

2. Arranging to get back any fees paid to her in advance.

3. Getting an itemized bill for any outstanding fees.

4. If your case is on contingency, discuss how she will be compensated. Usually your new attorney will pay your old attorney money from the case once it has been settled.

How to Dump 'Em

CLOSING ARGUMENT

If you're dealing with a lawyer you don't trust or who you think is overbilling you, lacks compassion, makes false promises, or handles your case in a way you don't agree with, and you've spoken with her about it and still nothing has changed, dump her. The good news: It's easier than you think. Lawyers deal with rejection on a daily basis, from losing cases to losing clients. Remember, time is money, so the longer you wait, the more legal fees you will be responsible for.

When firing your lawyer, back it up in writing. If you do it on the phone, as soon as you hang up the phone send her a certified letter confirming that the conversation took place. Clearly state that you will no longer need her services, and include the date on which you wish to terminate the relationship.

WHAT YOU CAN WRITE:

Dear _____,
As per our conversation on (insert date), effective (insert date), I will no longer be requiring your legal representation. Please forward my files to the following address (insert address).

Thank You,

_____

I OBJECT! AND SO DOES MY NEW LAWYER!

Too shy to dump your lawyer? Hire a new one and let her do it for you.

(MAL)PRACTICE MAKES PERFECT

Lawyers make mistakes; however, if you find that one mistake is followed by a slew of others, causing you to lose your case, you might want to consider a malpractice suit. Call a malpractice attorney if you feel that your lawyer was negligent in representing you or if you feel your lawyer acted unethically. File a complaint with your state's bar association and let it discipline your attorney. Go to www.abanet.org to find out which agencies deal with disciplining lawyers in your state. Be advised that although your lawyer may be punished for misconduct, it's difficult to recover money.

For those with issues regarding your lawyer's fees, consider fee arbitration. It's a good alternative to going to court, being less expensive and a whole lot quicker. Fee arbitration is run by your state or local bar association. Check out www.abanet.org for a list of state bar associations.

In a Pinch

DEFEND YOURSELF!

Tell your lawyer what a huge fan you are of law shows from *Perry Mason* to *Law & Order*. Then let her know that you've decided to defend yourself.

Thomas A. Mesereau Jr.

**HIGH-PROFILE DEFENSE LAWYER IN LOS ANGELES,
HAVING REPRESENTED MICHAEL JACKSON AND
ROBERT BLAKE AMONG MANY OTHERS.**

Q. *Why are people so intimidated by lawyers?*

A. First of all, most people only go to lawyers when they are in some kind of difficulty; that means they come in with a certain feeling of vulnerability. Additionally, many lawyers try to intimidate people because they know they are the only one that can save and protect their client. Lawyers spend three years in law school learning a language that very few people understand. They can intimidate by the very vocabulary they use. Our justice system can be scary to most individuals. People can lose their freedom, reputation, or financial security in a justice system run by lawyers and judges (most of whom are former lawyers).

Q. *Do you have any advice for people out there looking to hire a new lawyer?*

A. One should do everything possible to learn what reputation a lawyer has. The best people to talk to are lawyers and judges. Unfortunately, some lawyers are better marketers than they are lawyers. Conversely, some lawyers are excellent at what they do but are poor at marketing. Just because a lawyer has a name in the media doesn't mean they are any good. Don't let a lawyer prey on your vulnerabilities. For instance, if a lawyer guarantees a result, that could be a sign that they're unethical. Before my name became well known, I would often lose clients to other lawyers who made guarantees. I never make guarantees to a client because I think it's unprofessional and unethical. I've had potential clients get mad at me because I refused to give them a guarantee. When someone tells me another lawyer guaranteed them a result, I challenge them to get that lawyer to put it in writing. It never happens.

Q. *What are common mistakes people make with their lawyers?*
A. First of all, many people think their lawyer has only one case—namely their own. If a lawyer has only your case to deal with, then chances are they aren't very good. Good lawyers tend to be busy, so therefore don't get upset if a lawyer doesn't call you back immediately. Good lawyers will have numerous clients and responsibilities because they are in demand. Additionally, some people think they know more about what they require than their lawyer, so they start to tell them what to do. Just because a client has been very successful in their own business doesn't mean they are equally skilled in the legal profession. One should not hire a lawyer unless you want to listen to that lawyer's advice.

Q. *What are common mistakes lawyers make with their clients?*
A. Some lawyers give clients false hope by making them think they're winning when they're not. Others misrepresent what's actually going on for fear of being fired. And some lawyers will say anything to get a client, including lie about the law. Additionally, some lawyers are afraid to give the proper advice because they know other lawyers are telling the client what the client wants to hear.

Q. *If you suspect your lawyer is in a slump, how do you get them jazzed with your case?*
A. Sit them down and have a heart to heart with them. Be candid, and tell them all your concerns.

Q. *What are some reasons that someone should dump her lawyer?*
A. If they suspect that their lawyer is not doing the work they should be doing or if they feel they are being lied to. In both cases, having a heart to heart with your lawyer should take place.

Q. *What should a person do if there is a dispute over money?*
A. Discuss the issue with your lawyer; if you can't work it out, call your state bar association. Many have an arbitration program for resolving disputes between lawyers and clients.

Q. *What's the proper way to dump your lawyer?*
A. Tell your lawyer it isn't working out and confirm it in writing. You don't have to give reasons. Be sure you request all of your files in writing.

Q. *Can a lawyer dump their client?*
A. Sure. However, sometimes it takes permission from the court.

Q. *If you dump a lawyer, are they still bound by attorney-client privilege?*
A. Yes. Under federal and state laws, a lawyer must stay loyal to the client. However, if you sue your lawyer for malpractice, many of the confidential communications are no longer confidential, because the lawyer may have to explain what work they did.

Q. *What's the best way for people to prepare for court?*
A. Show respect for the court system and legal process. This means respecting everyone from the judge to the jury to the court personnel. And dress appropriately.

DUMPIPEDIA

▶ Hollywood criminal defense lawyer to the stars Robert Shapiro was dumped by legendary record producer Phil Spector (who was accused of killing B-movie actress Lana Clarkson). Spector claimed that Shapiro took unfair advantage of their personal friendship by trying to make money and garner publicity for himself.

▶ Sandra Day O'Connor was the first female lawyer to serve on the U.S. Supreme Court.

▶ "The first thing we do, let's kill all the lawyers" is Shakespeare's oft-quoted comment from *Henry VI, Part 2*.

▶ Steven Spielberg often called the shark in *Jaws* Bruce—the name of Spielberg's lawyer.

▶ Francis Scott Key, the man who wrote the words to "The Star-Spangled Banner," was a lawyer.

twenty-one

THE DOCTOR

Signs It's Time to Dump Your Doctor

▶ He asks you to pull his finger.

▶ He looks at your injury and says, "You should really see somebody about that."

▶ He faints at the sight of your blood.

▶ He says "whooopsie!" while examining you.

▶ He tells you it's time for a breast exam and shouts, "Yay! Boobies!"

▶ He points to a lump on his neck and asks, "Should I worry about this?"

It's Time for a Second Opinion

Last summer while at the beach, I slathered on sunscreen and noticed a small brown circle under my arm. Where did that come from?! Was that always there? How come I didn't notice it before? Freaking out, I pulled out the copy of *Los Angeles* magazine that I had in my beach bag. It was their annual "Best of Los Angeles" issue. I ripped that baby apart until I found the section on doctors. I quickly zeroed in on the dermatologist section, specifically the doctor who for three years in a row had been voted "Best Dermatologist to the Stars." Now I'm no star, but I figured this doctor must be good, because celebrities have very high standards. I immediately picked up the phone and called the office. Thankfully, all I had to do was mention the "C" word and they squeezed me in the very next day.

Doctor to the Stars had a very fancy office with a giant fish tank planted in the center of the waiting room. The receptionist handed me over twelve pages of paperwork and asked me to take a seat. Not long after that, a nurse escorted me to a sterile examining room and asked me to put on the paper gown that was folded on the examining table, and told me that the doctor would be right with me. By "right with me," she meant twenty-five minutes later. Twenty-five minutes of me obsessing about cancer and fidgeting with my paper gown, trying to figure out whether it was a dress or a shirt. I went with a dress and took my pants off—and then wished that I had worn nicer underwear. Then back to cancer. After a few minutes of deep breaths, I calmed down and started thinking about what my Doctor to the Stars might look like. I studied his diplomas on the wall and was pleased to discover that they were all from very good medical schools. I began picturing him looking like a young Cary Grant or George Clooney.

Strong, handsome, smart: Now I *really* wished that I had worn nicer underwear.

My fantasy was interrupted when the door opened and Doctor to the Stars rushed in; Cary Grant he was not. He scurried over to my face instead of my arm and spoke by rote, launching into a litany of the benefits of Botox and Restylane. He picked at my face for a few minutes. "Perfect!" he cried. "You're going to be so psyched when I'm done with you." Did he just say "psyched"?

As for my cancer fears? He barely glanced at my brown spot, assuring me that it was a sun spot. "Really? That's it? I was so worried," I said. "You sure?"

To which he annoyingly exhaled and said, "Fine, I'll take a picture of it if you want and then next time you come back, you can see if there are any changes. But I bet you there won't be." What was he, a five-year-old? He left the room and came back a moment later with a camera, then aggressively lifted my arm above my head and took pictures. When he was done he looked at my face—not my eyes—and said, "Now if you really want something to worry about, it should be whether you want to start with the V-beam laser for your broken capillaries or the IPL to smooth the surface of your face." And with that, I thanked him, put my clothes on, and left. I think I'll pass.

Doctor to the Stars was one of the easiest people I've had to break up with. His office, on the other hand, was a different story. By the time I got home, my inbox was flooded with e-mails from his office about special offers on laser treatments, hair removal, and Botox. It even put me on the e-mail list for his partner, a gastroenterologist. I begged his office to remove my e-mail address from its system, but it never did. It seemed as though the more I called the office, begging it to stop, the more phone calls I received asking me when I was going to make my next appointment. I have a pretty good suspicion that the *Los Angeles* magazine writer who did the story on Doctor to the Stars made some kind of deal with his office—if she included him in her "Best of" list, her name would be removed from its system. Lucky girl.

What I Learned

I'm a scaredy cat when it comes to dealing with doctors. I'd rather get punched in the boob than have someone stick a needle in me—just writing the word "needle" makes my mouth warm and my underarms sweat. I talked to a lot of patients, doctors, and nurses for this chapter, and what I discovered was that the best doctor-patient relationships are formed when both parties share responsibility in making decisions and planning the patient's course of treatment. Surprisingly, many people (including myself) show up, listen to the doctor, and do everything he says without so much as questioning it. I didn't go to medical school—what do I know? But the truth is, I know a lot more than I think I do.

Writing this chapter inspired me to go online and research medical information relevant to my history. I even started a file on my computer with medical Web site addresses and wrote down questions to ask my doctor. The old me always thought that I'd remember my questions. Although I have a good memory in my everyday life, the second I walk into a doctor's office, I go blank. I'm lucky if I can remember my name; let alone my family's medical history. One doctor I spoke to actually keeps notepads in his examining room so patients can write down questions.

This chapter motivated me to actually find a new doctor. I asked everyone I knew who they went to and narrowed my list. Then I called the doctors' offices and spoke to the staff. It's amazing how much information staff can provide—everything from average wait times to your doctor's bedside manner. It was important to me to find a patient doctor who listens and shows compassion. If I feel rushed, I get flustered. In the end, I found the perfect doctor for me: Dr. Edison DeMello in Santa Monica, California. My first visit to Dr. DeMello lasted two hours. By the end of the appointment, he knew the names of all my family members. He made it his goal to listen to and connect with me, and it worked. I asked questions, and he answered using a language and tone that really resonated with me. He also insisted I call him if I had other questions when I got home. Do doctors still scare me? You betcha. But by empowering myself with knowledge, I've managed to eliminate most of my fear. They may have gone to medical school, but I wrote a book!

Laying the Groundwork

▶ Find out whether your doctor has had any disciplinary actions filed against him. Check out www.castleconnelly.com for links to all fifty states' medical boards.

▶ Call your doctor's office and ask his staff how your doctor prefers to handle termination. If they advise you to drop by for an office visit, do so—just be sure that you won't get charged for it.

▶ Line up another doctor before dumping your current one. Ask around for referrals. If you still need help, go to www.WebMd .com. Or for unbiased doctor reviews, check out www .AngiesList.com; it relies on its members to submit reviews and allows the doctor to respond. Submissions are examined by the staff at Angie's List, and are investigated when necessary.

▶ Make a point of not burning bridges. You never know when or if you're going to need something from your old doctor.

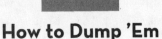

How to Dump 'Em

FINAL CHECKUP

The ideal relationship with a doctor should be one in which you and your doctor work out your course of treatment. Handing control over to one's doctor leaves patients feeling powerless. If you're not satisfied for any reason with your doctor, write him a polite letter. Explain that you're changing doctors and include as much information as possible, such as your address, phone number, and the name of your new physician.

WHAT YOU CAN WRITE:

> *Dear Dr. _____,*
> *After careful consideration I've decided to change doctors. As of (insert date), I will be a patient of Dr. _____. Please forward all my medical records, including X-rays and lab reports, to the following address _____.*
> > *Thank You,*
> > _____

HAVE YOUR NEW DOCTOR DO IT FOR YOU

Dump your doctor by having your new one do it for you. With your permission, your new doctor's office can call your old physician and request your medical records.

THE PLANS, THEY ARE A-CHANGIN'

The U.S. health care system is in serious crisis, with the U.S. Census Bureau reporting that 47 million Americans are uninsured. Explain to your doctor that you either changed insurance plans and that his office is not covered under your new policy, or that you temporarily don't have insurance.

<hr>

In a Pinch

I'VE GOT A CRUSH ON YOU
Tell your doctor that you're terribly embarrassed, but that you have a giant crush on him. Let him know that you were trying to work through it in therapy, but unfortunately it's so overwhelming that you absolutely must switch doctors. Tread carefully or be prepared for him to ask you out.

GUESS WHO FOUND RELIGION?
Christian Scientists believe that God denies sin, sickness, death, and the material world. Adherents often refuse traditional medical treatments. Why not tell your doctor that you found religion—and it doesn't have room for doctors. Your life is now in God's hands, not his.

Q&A

Dr. Jason Gonsky

ASSISTANT PROFESSOR OF MEDICINE,
DIVISION OF HEMATOLOGY AND ONCOLOGY
SUNY Downstate Medical Center and Kings County Hospital Center

Q. *Why do you think it's so difficult for a patient to dump a doctor?*

A. Probably because you've made a connection of some sort. You may have opened up in a way that was difficult, revealed something that made you feel vulnerable, or established a relationship based on trust and understanding. These connections are hard to walk away from without fear or a sense of loss. Or you may just have a crush on him. I'm told this happens.

Q. *How do you dump your doctor?*

A. If you haven't established a good relationship, just ask the office manager for a copy of your records and find a new one. If you do have a connection with your doctor, but after careful consideration you feel it would be best to transfer your care to somebody else, at your next appointment just tell your doctor you will be transferring your care. Ask if there's anything special you should tell the new doctor. If you have any chronic conditions that the doctor is managing, ask her to draft a letter for the new doctor (at her convenience) and ask the office manager for a copy of your records. If you feel like discussing your reasons, do so. If not, don't worry. Chances are your doctor has many, many patients, and your loss won't weigh on his or her mind for long. If it does and you are leaving for cause, perhaps it will prompt some reflection.

Q. *When dumping your doctor, is it best to do it in person, on the telephone, or by letter?*

A. For most doctors, telephone calls are tough. When you call the office, the doctor will most likely be with a patient and will have to call back—maybe at a time that's not convenient for you. Then there's the potential for real awkwardness. If you feel there's something you need to say and you express yourself best in writing, a letter can work well. Just be sure you don't write anything you might regret. If there are no hard feelings, just break up in person at your next appointment.

Q. *What's the best way for a patient to bring up an issue he's having with his doctor?*

A. If there's an issue you want to discuss, you should let your doctor know at the beginning of the appointment. Because of scheduling and time constraints, different doctors handle these issues in different ways. Ask your doctor what is the best way to discuss your issue. He might want to address it at the end of the appointment, over the phone after office hours, by e-mail, or at the next appointment, depending on the frequency of your visits. If your doctor doesn't have time or won't make time to discuss it, that's a problem.

Q. *What do you tell people who are deathly afraid of going to the doctor?*

A. They're talking to one. I try to figure out why they're so afraid and then decide if it is really important for them to go at that time. Some are afraid of being told officially they are sick. If they avoid the doctor, the tumor, the pain, the headaches, the rashes— whatever—can be ignored and denied. Some are afraid of being chastised for their obesity, lack of exercise, or poor adherence to a plan of care. A doctor is an authority figure they don't want criticizing them. Some had bad experiences when they were young and afraid and powerless, and associate that fear with the doctor. Some just fear the possibility of illness being discovered.

Q. *What's the biggest misconception people have about doctors?*
A. That we are all the same. There are a lot of doctors.

Q. *What's the most common mistake patients make with their doctor?*
A. Thinking your doctor can read your mind, thinking there's an easy solution or a pill for every problem, not taking enough responsibility for your own role in your care, and assuming your appointment will be exactly on time. Always bring something to read. Don't think your doctor is an idiot if he can't tell you immediately what's wrong with you.

Q. *What irritates you the most about patients?*
A. I really go out of my way to help my patients, so I get irritated when patients repeatedly don't listen, disregard my advice, or fail to follow up out of laziness. I sometimes get a little irritated when patients wait until the end of the appointment and pull an "Oh, by the way, I'm losing a lot of blood when I go to the bathroom lately. . . . " Waiting 'till the last minute to bring up the real problem wastes a ton of time.

Q. *Does an apple a day really keep the doctor away?*
A. It does if you keep throwing it at him.

DUMPIPEDIA

▶ Isaiah Washington, the actor who played Dr. Burke on TV's *Grey's Anatomy*, was dumped for uttering a homosexual slur toward a castmate.

▶ A spin doctor is a person who publicizes favorable interpretations of the words and actions of a public figure, especially a politician.

▶ Doctors Without Borders is an international medical humanitarian organization created by doctors to serve people threatened by violence, neglect, or catastrophe.

▶ William Henry Harrison was the only U.S. president who studied to become a doctor.

▶ According to *The Guinness Book of World Records*, Balamurali Ambati is the youngest person ever to become a doctor. He graduated New York University at the age of thirteen and Mount Sinai School of Medicine when he was twenty.

▶ On which of the following shows did *Desperate Housewives* star Marcia Cross not play a doctor?
   A. *Seinfeld*
   B. *Everwood*
   C. *Ally McBeal*
   D. *Melrose Place*

The correct answer is C. Ally McBeal.
Marcia played an architect accused of sexual harassment.

twenty-two

THE MECHANIC

Signs It's Time to Dump Your Mechanic

▶ He asks *you* what that clanking sound is.

▶ You ask whether he has a license—and he shows you his driver's license.

▶ He slides under your car with a wrench in one hand and a how-to guide in the other.

▶ His hands are clean and his nails are newly manicured.

▶ He tells you that he can't service your car because he doesn't know how to drive a stick shift.

Putting the Brakes on Your Mechanic

Before moving to Los Angeles, I knew nothing about mechanics or cars, for that matter. I bought the safest vehicle I knew, a brand new Volvo, and naively thought that I would never need a mechanic. I figured that my car had a warranty, so if something went wrong, I'd bring it back to the Volvo dealership and let them take care of it. Once the warranty ran out, I'd just dump the old car and buy a new one.

Things didn't exactly go as I planned. Within a few months of buying my car, I heard a crash outside of a friend's house. I ran to see what happened and that's when I met Clara, an elderly woman who had backed into the side of my car while pulling out of her driveway. I could tell how awful she felt. Tears were shed, hugs were exchanged, and neither one of us could believe that any of this was happening. It was clear that she had made a mistake, and so knowing this, she begged me not to go through her insurance company, since her rate would go up drastically and she could barely manage to afford it now. I accepted that and promised her that I would find a reasonably priced mechanic.

His name was Mani Mol. A good friend recommended him, telling me that he was great and cheap. Mani was a short, slender, middle-aged Indian man who wore a maroon Members Only jacket and a black toupee that was at least two sizes too big for his head, so had a disturbing habit of sliding around, but he had a kind face. After I told him Clara's story, he looked at my car, assessed the damage, and told me he would do it for $500 in cash. Done.

All was right with the world—until I showed up a week later to pick up my car at the garage. My silver Volvo, which had a thin black bumper running along the driver's and rear passenger's side, was now drenched in silver paint. So was the side-view mirror—only that looked more like he used silver spray paint, the kind taggers use to graffiti warehouse walls. I pointed it out to Mani, who genuinely looked surprised before saying, "No problem, no problem. Come back tomorrow."

But when I came back the following day, he had taken what I can only assume was a razor blade to my bumper. My poor Volvo looked like it been in a street fight. Upon closer inspection of the rest of the door, the dent was still totally noticeable, even creating a rippling effect. Mani still looked clueless and said, "Looks good, no?" Uhmmm, no!

I was in trouble. But it had been my choice to use Mani; I had already accepted Clara's cash. This was my problem now. Each time I returned to Mani's shop, I was met with the same clueless expression. He couldn't see the horrible job he did. The rippling? "Reflection from another car." Gashes in my bumper? "What gashes?" The only thing he copped to was the overspray on the side-view mirror to which he said, "Whoops!"

That was it, I had to dump him. Since I had no idea what kind of additional damage he had done to my car, I drove to another repair shop. The technician there told me Mani did way more damage to my car than Clara had done initially. He informed me that it was going to cost three times the amount that Mani charged. I rang Mani with the information and asked only that he give me my money back. When he refused, I told him I would see him in court.

Mani brought two other members of the Members Only club with him to court for emotional support. The judge only had to take one look at my poor car parked in front of the courthouse steps and he immediately understood. "This looks awful!" said the judge. He then turned to Mani and asked him what he had to say for himself.

"What? It's good. If you say it's not good, then it's not good. My bad."

That was followed by the judge's ruling: "Judgment for the plaintiff, $1,600."

What I Learned

I'm the kind of girl who waits for a light to appear on her dashboard before taking her car in. I'll drive on tires that are completely bald and have no idea that anything's wrong until they either fall off my car or someone says something. I dreaded writing this chapter because I had so little experience with cars and mechanics. I realize now what a fool I was for choosing a mechanic based on his bargain rates, even if it was to help an elderly woman out. Researching mechanics is important. There are tons of Web sites that rate mechanics in your area; use them.

My favorite story that I heard while researching this chapter came from a friend of a friend of mine. She took her car into the shop for a bulb change and was told by her mechanic that it would cost $40–50 max to replace. When she went to pick her car up a few hours later, the bill was $400. Shocked, she asked what the extra $350 was for. He told her he needed to replace the flux capacitor. She nodded her head and left. When she told her husband that night, he hit the roof. The flux capacitor? It's the name of the device responsible for time travel in the movie *Back to the Future*. The mechanic returned their money and confessed that he had earned a good amount of money over the years using that one. I bet.

It was shocking to discover how many complaints have been filed with the Better Business Bureau accusing mechanics of charging for labor and repairs that were never actually done. I'm doing my research from now on so I don't find myself face to face with another Mani Mol.

Common Mechanic Cons

1. Telling you that your brakes are going to give out at any minute.

2. Loosening your spark plug cables and then charging you to tighten them. Be sure to check them yourself.

3. Pouring antifreeze on your alternator, causing it to give off smoke while the engine is hot—then telling you that your car needs a lot of repairs.

4. Charging you for a new part but using a spare one—or worse yet, not changing it at all. Ca-ching! Avoid this by asking to see your old part and the new part.

5. Charging you for brand-name parts but actually using knock-off parts made in China.

6. Checking your oil by only dipping the stick in halfway—and then charging you for an entire bottle of oil and labor.

7. Putting a hole in your tire. The mechanic stabs your tire with a nail and then tells you that it's time to buy a new one.

How to Save Money

1. Learn to communicate with your mechanic. When your car stops running smoothly, do you know how to tell your mechanic what's going on? For instance, when your car stalls, do you walk into your mechanic's garage and say, "My car's not working"? Learn to be specific. When does it stall? While you're driving? Only when you stop? If your car makes strange clicking sounds, when do you hear them? Only when you're turning? If

your car shakes, does it happen on surface streets, or only on the highway? Also, be sure to tell your mechanic about the related driving conditions. Was it raining or snowing when you heard that humming sound? How about the air conditioning—was it on? The more details you can provide, the better.

2. Educate yourself. Buy a book, ask a friend, call a mechanic. Get to know your car.

3. Choose the right kind of shop. Warranty work should be taken straight to the dealer. However, if your car is not under warranty, think twice before taking your car there, as prices tend to be much higher. Chains offer routine repairs such as brakes, tires, batteries, mufflers, and oil changes, but don't always have the best-trained mechanics. If you do go to a chain, make sure it's one that specializes in the repair you need. Your best bet is finding an independent mechanic. He may charge more, but if you find one you trust, you'll most likely save money in the long run.

4. Next time your car is at the shop, ask questions. Force your mechanic to be as specific as possible about the work he's going to do. The more involved you are, the less money you will likely have to pay.

5. After your mechanic gives you an estimate, tell him you'd like to call a few other mechanics to compare prices. Some will lower their estimates after hearing that. One guy I interviewed had a "check engine" light illuminated on his dashboard and went to his mechanic to have him turn it off. The mechanic wanted to charge him $500. He called another mechanic who charged $60. When I got my settlement from my case against Mani, I went to an auto body shop to get a quote for the job. The mechanic quoted me a price of $3,200. The shop down the street quoted me a rate of just $1,200.

6. Tell your mechanic up front that you want to see the old parts if anything needs to be replaced. Some shady mechanics will charge you for new parts and never install them.

Laying the Groundwork

▶ Collect all your written paperwork including estimates, cost of parts, labor, and so forth.

▶ Read the fine print at your mechanic's garage. Make sure to read all signs on the walls and counters. You might need this information if you need to take your mechanic to court.

▶ Familiarize yourself with your state laws. Many states prohibit mechanics from charging more than 10 percent above the price stated in the original estimate. They're also prevented from working on your car without oral consent. Call or check out the Department of Consumer Affairs and find out more info.

▶ If you suspect you're dealing with a shady mechanic, call 1-877-FTC-HELP and have the Federal Trade Commission help you. It works with consumers to prevent fraud and deceptive and unfair business practices, as well as providing useful information on the spot.

▶ Find a new mechanic. Check out CarTalk.com and Mechanics NearYou.com. These two sites help consumers find reputable local mechanics.

Tip: When possible, make sure your mechanic has been certified by the ASE (National Institute for Automotive Service Excellence). For more information, check out www .asecert.org.

How to Dump 'Em

TAKE THE HIGH ROAD

Dump your mechanic by writing him a letter or calling and speaking to him in person—or you can always leave a message on his machine.

> **WHAT YOU SAY:** *"Hi, it's (insert your name). I want to thank you for all your years of service. I'm calling to let you know that I felt it was time for a change, so I decided to take my car to a new shop (closer to home?). Thanks again for everything."*

DIY MECHANIC

Interested in saving money? Learn how to be your own mechanic, and dump your old one by letting him know that you're going to be doing your own work from now on. You can save thousands of dollars by learning the most basic of automotive checkups. And the best part is, a lot of it's actually easy. Check out About.com's auto repair section. It offers a DIY repairs section where you can learn how to fix the easiest problems while getting instructions on how to handle advanced tasks. It also has an auto repair expert whom you can e-mail at autorepair.guide@about.com. Another site to check out for interesting articles and personalized automotive advice is www.askamechanic.info.

SPECIALIST

Dump your mechanic by letting him know that you're going to go to a mechanic who specializes in your kind of car.

In a Pinch

NEW WHEELS

Tell your mechanic that you bought a brand new car and that it has the most amazing warranty. It includes everything!

I WANT TO RIDE MY BICYCLE

Who needs a car when you can ride a bicycle? Tell your mechanic that you got rid of your car and have decided to rely on your bicycle for transportation. You can also use taxis, limos, or share-a-rides as an alternative.

Billy Stabile

OWNER OF STABILE AUTOMOTIVE IN LOS ANGELES.

Billy has provided cars for over twenty years to films and television shows, including The 40-Year-Old Virgin, Evan Almighty, and Happy Days. He's also my mechanic.

Q. *How do you know when it's time to put the brakes on your mechanic?*
A. When he leaves love notes in your glove box.

Q. *How do you dump your mechanic?*
A. Intimidation. Tell him you're going to night classes and you now know everything.

Q. *What should someone do if he thinks his mechanic is overcharging him?*
A. Tell them you called around and found their prices to be much higher. They don't need to know the only person you actually called is your mother, asking her, "What's for dinner?"

Q. *What's the biggest mistake people make when it comes to their cars?*
A. They don't pay attention to basic maintenance issues—like driving around with not enough air in the tires or low oil under the hood.

Q. *What's the most common thing people come to you for that you know they can do or fix themselves?*
A. Windshield washer fluid.

Q. *On the flip side, what's the one thing people think they can do or fix themselves but should leave to their mechanic?*
A. Brakes. It's not something you want to take the chance on. But then again, it's more money for the auto body guys.

Q. *What's the biggest scam people should be on the lookout for when it comes to mechanics?*
A. Belts and hoses. Very rarely do they need to be replaced, so if your mechanic is insisting on it, get a second opinion.

Q. *What's the most important thing a person should look for when hiring a mechanic?*
A. Cleanliness, reputation, and zodiac sign.

Q. *Chain or private shop?*
A. A private shop has a lot more to lose; it's do or die for them, whereas a chain mechanic is going to be getting a paycheck at the end of the week no matter what.

Q. *Why do so many mechanics hang girly pictures on their walls?*
A. Because we can only fit so many of them in our wallets.

DUMPIPEDIA

▶ Enzo Ferrari was a mechanic before he created the Ferrari car.

▶ In a 2007 Gallup poll, only 25 percent of Americans said that they thought that auto mechanics have high ethical standards.

▶ According to AAA, the Federal Trade Commission estimates that Americans spend billions of dollars each year on fraudulent or unneeded auto repairs.

▶ CarTalk.com did a survey and discovered that dealerships charge on average 15 percent more than independent repair shops for the same repair.

▶ Evangeline Lilly once worked as a mechanic.

▶ Mike+The Mechanics was an English rock/pop band started in 1985 by one of the founding members of the band Genesis, Mike Rutherford. They are perhaps best known for their single, "All I Need Is a Miracle."

dumping your author

Thank you for reaching this point. I'm so happy that you didn't dump me in the middle of the book; I would have been terribly disappointed. But proud, too . . . had you done it properly.

Here are some basic strategic points to bolster your skills. We'll use the example of you dumping me as our final exercise.

1. **Write down the list of reasons you want to dump me.** Writing things out unearths latent thoughts and feelings. Then walk away and come back to it later. Maybe you thought you wanted to dump me, but actually you just needed some time to cool off. For example, you're writing your list of reasons to dump me, and suddenly your stomach starts to hurt. Furiously scribbling away, you recall a memory of being teased by a girl on the playground when you were little whose name was also Jodyne. It was so bad that you had to transfer schools.

2. **Give me a warning and perhaps offer a suggestion.** Make it clear that if things don't change, you will have to dump me. You could say, *"I had a bad experience when I was a child with a girl named Jodyne. Tears were shed. Bruises were had. Let's just leave it at that. There was a teacher named Miss Cindy who held*

me when I cried. Would you change your name to Miss Cindy? If you can't, I will have to find another author to read."

3. **If I don't change my name, it's time to dump me.** Start by practicing what you're going to say to me. Plan it out. Maybe start by looking at my picture on the back of my book. Prop it up against a pillow and rehearse. *"Jodyne, I found your advice ___."*

4. **Dump me.** If possible, do me the courtesy of dumping me in person. Your goal is to remain calm and in control of yourself. Speak clearly and directly while delivering your message. Remember, less is more, so try hard not to get emotionally involved. Start with a compliment or say something positive; a compliment has a wonderful way of softening the blow. You could say, *"Jodyne, I was impressed by how many pages were in your book. However, I find your decision to keep your name personally offensive."*

5. **Allow me to respond or have a reaction.** *"Unfortunately I'm not willing to change my name to Miss Cindy, because I have a lifetime of being called Jodyne and a career under that name. You may call me Miss Jody. Would that work?"*

6. **Stand firm in your decision.** *"I appreciate your willingness to allow me to call you Miss Jody, but unfortunately, it's not enough. At this point, I would feel more comfortable reading someone else's how-to book. Good luck with any future books you may write. I will not read them."*

Yay! You did it. You dumped me. Nice work. My job here is done.

Finally, if I did not include your specific breakup in this book, I'm sorry. I meant to, really. At least now you're armed with tools and information to apply as needed. When done right, dumping someone means taking control of a situation instead of letting the situation control you. Congratulations on having successfully mastered the art of the breakup. So what are you waiting for? Get out there and dump 'em!

acknowledgments

Thank you, Kimmie Auerbach, for encouraging me to write the proposal and for sharing your agent with me, the lovely and amazing Elisabeth Weed at Weed Literary. As a writer, if you're lucky, you land one editor; I was fortunate enough to have two. Kathy Huck, thank you for picking me and bringing me to the folks at HarperCollins. And Matthew Benjamin, you're by no means a sloppy second. Your humor, strength, and ability to rein me in when necessary were greatly appreciated.

With gratitude to my dear friends Kathleen Beaton, Michael Hawley, Lori Levine, Leslie Appelbaum, David Christensen, Natalie Caplan, Ellen Schinderman, Cherryl Hanson, Brad Listi, and Rich Ferguson, who never complained when I forced them to read chapters—and force them I did. Thank you, Bret Shuckis, for being such a great cheerleader; Nick Smith for your awesome letters; Eric Keyes for being there in my eleventh hour; and to Michelle Boyaner for staring at fonts with me until we were cross-eyed. To the talented artist Julie Bossinger, thank you for your amazingly funny illustrations. Anyone reading this should buy her artwork at www.JuliesArt.com immediately. Eternal thanks to all those who graciously participated in the Q&A chapters: Bob Harper, Thomas Mesereau, Aggie Mackenzie, Adam

Carolla, Kato Kaelin, Paul-Jean Jouve, Darlene Basch, Bruce Miller, Alexandra Levit, Billy Stabile, Katie Vaughan, Susie Stein, Guy Stilson, and Dr. Jason Gonsky.

To my family, Phil and Mikie Speyer, Donald and Janice Silverman: I'm not sure you really understood what I was writing, but you loved and supported me anyway. And to my sissies, Susan, Laura, and Sarah Silverman, thank you for your love, support and advice. And finally, to all the people that I've encountered over the years who have inspired me to explore and master the art of the dump, thank you. Hopefully I've been able to teach future generations of dumpers how to do it better.

about the author

Jodyne L. Speyer is a recovering avoidant who lives and works in Los Angeles. She has produced documentaries for National Geographic and has worked on such shows as *Joe Millionaire*, *Shear Genius*, and *The Supreme Court of Comedy*. She has successfully dumped hundreds of people, not all of them on her own behalf.